**Praise for Love, If That's **

"Marijke Schermer flawlessly analyzes how
love takes its course."
Het Parool

"On every page Schermer excels with sentences
that seem ordinary, but are packed with meaning.
After every striking sentence, I had to put the
book down for a while."
Trouw

"Schermer's technical ingenuity traps you,
making you question your standards, assumptions,
and blind spots. This is a big and definitive, but
also investigative, story about love. Schermer
is one of the most interesting writers in the
Netherlands."
NRC Handelsblad

"*Love, If That's What It Is* has the potential to
become as successful as Herman Koch's *The Dinner*."
De Standaard

"Schermer zooms in on the essential question of
how autonomous you can still be when you live
together. This novel has a careful and poetic style

and is precise in its construction. Schermer effortlessly manages to infect you with the feelings of the novel's characters. *Love, If That's What It Is* paws and tugs at your fixed concepts."
Tzum

"Schermer's fresh style adds something really new to the mountain of stories about falling in love, unhappy marriages, cheating, and heart-break—she seems to have cleared the dust of the whole theme."
De Volkskrant

"Stories about love and relationships have often been told, but Schermer's approach to these themes puts it all into a new light and cannot be compared with that of any other writer. Her work has been compared with Ian McEwan's, though, in which often a wrong step or decision radically alters a life for good."
Literair Nederland

"With *Love, If That's What It Is*, Marijke Schermer wrote a modern tale of love and the (im)possi-bility of a happy marriage."
deBuren

Love,
if that's what it is

Marijke Schermer

Love,
if that's what it is

Translated from the Dutch
by Hester Velmans

WORLD EDITIONS

New York, London, Amsterdam

Published in the USA in 2022 by World Editions LLC, New York
Published in the UK in 2022 by World Editions Ltd., London

World Editions
New York / London / Amsterdam

Copyright © Marijke Schermer, 2019
First Published by Uitgeverij Van Oorschot, Netherlands
English translation copyright © Hester Velmans, 2022
Author portrait © Annaleen Louwes

Printed by Lake Book, USA

World Editions is committed to a sustainable future. Papers used by
World Editions meet the FSC standards of certification.

This book is a work of fiction. Any resemblance to actual persons,
living or dead, or actual events is purely coincidental. The opinions
expressed therein are those of the characters and should not be confused with those of the author.

Library of Congress Cataloging in Publication Data is available

ISBN 978-1-64286-103-7

First published as *Liefde, als dat het is* by Uitgeverij Van Oorschot,
Netherlands

Published by special arrangement with Uitgeverij Van Oorschot
in conjunction with their duly appointed agent 2 Seas Literary
Agency

This publication has been made possible with financial support
from the Dutch Foundation for Literature

N ederlands
letterenfonds
dutch foundation
for literature

Twitter: @WorldEdBooks
Facebook: @WorldEditionsInternationalPublishing
Instagram: @WorldEdBooks
YouTube: World Editions
www.worldeditions.org

Book Club Discussion Guides are available on our website.

SUMMER

Outside the tie that binds

It's always the same thing, more or less: they exchange a few words, they have a beer or a tonic or a glass of water, sometimes he'll take a shower, and then they go to bed. It's just the right balance of levity and gravity. It's exciting, uninhibited, but also emotional. Sometimes he winds up sobbing in her arms. Afterwards they lie back and relax. Sometimes they drowse off a bit. They talk about their jobs, about their kids, he talks about the disaster, she comes to his wife's defense. During dinner they gaze out at the view. Sev lives on a high floor, you can see the city from her window, and the way the river snakes through it. Then, if there's time, they'll go back to bed. He always comes empty-handed: no wine, no flowers. He never stays the night. He always says it's the last time. She calls a cab for him and then watches from above as he gets in and is driven off.

The balcony doors are open but the curtain is drawn against the heat of the sun. Sev, leaning back against the kitchen sink in the semidarkness, sends David a text. She pictures him in his own house, where she has never been, in the kitchen. The way he deals with his despair by taking care of his daughters. The way they put up with it, old enough to make up their own minds. She has never met them; all she knows about them, about him and his wife, is what he's told her. She uses her imagination.

She, for her part, dropped off Hendrik, her eight-year-old, at his dad's this afternoon. The sense of space the prospect of a week's freedom gives her is mixed with a vague sense of loss. She waits for David to read her words and let her know they have hit home, she knows her words do that, that's the reason she sends them. The wireless audio system floods the rooms of her apartment with the sounds of Satie. David says his marriage was happy for twenty-five years, that his life was happy until the disaster struck. She grabs a beer, considers what to eat: something spicy, something child-unfriendly. She empties her briefcase on the table, she can get some work done later, when it's a little cooler. Twenty-five years of bliss in smithereens; Sev doesn't know which is more mystifying to her—those twenty-five years, or the final deathblow.

The screen on her phone lights up with the word *Stomach*. She smiles. Twenty-four hours from now David will run his hands over her body. That was what it was about, her message, about those hands: that she can already feel them, and where. She thinks of the first time, when they had sex before she'd ever seen his face or heard his voice. A meticulously prearranged event; she'd detailed every step he was to take when he got to her place. She had described what they were going to do, what she would do, what she expected of him. In the rapidly shortening countdown to his arrival, it had crossed her mind that, despite their dating correspondence, she really didn't know a thing about him. When she went out to buy wine that afternoon, it occurred to her that he might be a seedy type with foamy spittle at the corners of his mouth clutching a bottle of vodka. She'd thought to herself: a serial killer would never have wasted so many words on getting to know her, or gone into such elaborate detail; would never have delivered his lines so passionately or persuasively. She was strong, in good shape, she was no victim, she could always hide a knife under the bed.

When he stepped into her darkened bedroom, silhouetted in the doorway, she thought: a man, he's not a boy, but a man. He took off his shoes, his shirt and his pants next to the bed, she could smell him, he slipped under the thin covers and laid his head on her breast.

Next comes a photo of his frying pan. He often sends pictures of the food he's preparing. She zooms in on what's in the background, tries to complete the puzzle with incidental things, the herbs he's using, the stuff he buys, the knives he's cutting with, his kids' clutter, the trivialities of domestic life he is keeping from her. She is suddenly in the mood for shrimp.

He has never told her she's beautiful, or mentioned anything he thinks is beautiful about her. She likes it that way. She's had boyfriends who thought she was pretty, and boyfriends who didn't think she was pretty enough. Those kinds of appraisals, even if positive, are always demeaning. The way he looks at her when he touches her, the way he lies back and surrenders to her, the way he tucks into the food she cooks for him and tells her about his life, that's what it's about, for her. He says her unconventional conduct and independence of spirit are a way of shielding herself from the judgment of others. He says he envies her her freedom. He says it's not that she's incapable of having a real relationship, as she once suggested, but that she simply doesn't *want* one. It's in his misconceptions about her that his admiration shines through. She snaps a picture of her bottle of beer, writes something about his tongue and about his head between her thighs. She wants to unsettle him, the devoted dad.

She has known him for four months and hasn't ever been with him in the company of other people, has never met anyone from his life, has never been seen in public with him. Is that a good way of getting to know each other? Or does it obscure other aspects of his personality that could be just as revealing? At a party, he probably wouldn't be the one she'd have picked. In her circle of friends, she'd have pegged him as Terri's guy. He is well spoken and capable of reasoned thought, she knows he isn't a blowhard, that he is witty and quick on the uptake, that he reads books and follows the news and that his political opinions diverge from hers only in a few instances, making for stimulating discussion. But she also thinks she knows how reserved he normally is in company, she knows how totally wrapped up in his family he'd become, which comes with something inherent to the nuclear family—something impregnable. There is something they leave at home, something they don't need in the confrontation with the outside world; something that doesn't have to be proved or justified to anyone else. It is precisely for that reason that they could not have met each other at any other time than at the nadir of his crisis. It's because his inner world was tucked away so securely for so long, all its turbulence buried under contentment, self-control and moral principle, that it is now, laid bare in the eye of the storm, a dazzling pearl. She simply can't get enough of it.

He says she has opened up a whole new world for him. Sev worries that he means just the sex, but only when she allows herself to be the least noble incarnation of herself. The truth is that all those different compartments can't be disconnected: sex, love, intimacy, understanding, nostalgia. The trouble is that they aren't disconnected. *Just this, you and me, and this island in time ...* She doesn't know if she can stick to that arrangement.

David, in his kitchen, minces the garlic, the peppers, the shallots, and slides them into the oil. Love. He pats the shrimp dry and tosses the spaghetti in the boiling water. Love. He sautés the parsley briefly in the small frying pan and chucks the shrimp into another pan. Love of his children. He pours a glass of wine down his throat. Twice the love, twice the worries. Anything they need, he'll give them, and more. His shirt is plastered to his back. He pours himself another glass. From the day Terri entered his life, twenty-five years ago, *he* and *she* gradually changed into *we*, and in the second decade of their union, that *we* ballooned into the collective of a family, that many-headed organism. *He* and *she* dissolved and disappeared, like waves in the sea. Which is why he hasn't the foggiest who he is now; he only knows *where* he is: here, in his house. The flash of surprise on Sev's face whenever he says that sort of thing. He picks some basil leaves from the plant on the windowsill. The window is dingy, he should clean it when the sunlight is gone. The ball of mozzarella on the counter makes him think of her naked body. He shudders. He gives the pasta pot's lid a twist just in time to prevent it boiling over. He gets the right knife ready. He cooks the way he fixes things, a spark of inspiration followed by a strict series of precision moves.

When Ally asked Terri to *stop hurting Daddy*, he was struck by the sensation of the world heeling over in the wrong direction. As if his children had to protect *him*, instead of the other way around. But then it dawned on him that it was something else entirely. In the cesspit of misery their life had become, it wasn't about protecting or being protected. He and Krista and Ally were one body, one organ, and when Ally had mentioned his hurt, it was also her own pain. But the love, the care and the spaghetti will hide the pain, and make it go away. They'll not want for anything, anything at all. Theirs will be a house filled with life, affection, and joy. Now that they no longer have to come up to Terri's high expectations, it will even be easier to achieve than before. Now that it's no longer such a pity that Krista is no longer on the advanced track, or that Ally has been placed into the general rather than the Latin and Greek stream; now that he is no longer expected to engage in all sorts of self-improvement—jogging, learning something new, a language, a musical instrument, the demeaning nature of her suggestions—now that he can do as he pleases, and the children can be their not-particularly-gifted selves, happiness may be closer than ever before. Actually, it's better this way. Actually, it's a mystery why he always tried so hard to accommodate her wishes. It's only now, now that it's no longer necessary, that he recognizes the contortions he used to put himself through, and how laid-back he is now, or is on the way to becoming, anyway. He sweeps the parings and crumbs from the counter into his open palm and drops them into the gleaming cylindrical—terribly inconvenient (he hears her say it)—garbage can. He cuts his finger on the serrated knife he's using for the tomatoes. For an instant, just before he drops the knife and the pain begins to register, he wonders what would happen if he sawed right through to the bone. Blood starts to drip onto the cutting board, running into the juice from the tomatoes, until he puts his finger in his mouth. He tastes the iron, his saliva makes the wound sting. He feels a yawning emptiness sneaking up on him from within. He wants to shout: This wasn't the deal! This isn't the fucking deal we had!

He sets the table with forks and knives. A fleeting memory—their search for a table, the perfect dining table, a table to go with the house, all the talk that went into it, all the deliberations with her, with other people, but with her especially. He moves the newspaper aside. *Heat wave persists* glares the headline on the front page, which ripples in the breeze of the fan. A glance through the half-closed curtains at the deserted street— the harsh white light, the air shimmering just above the hot asphalt, the jumbled lines of the paving stones: hopscotch chalk, a memory that's gone before he can grasp it. His hands on the tabletop. Hands that don't really seem to go with the rest of his body, Sev once said. Hands that now leave a smudge of blood. He hunts for Band-Aids in the dresser drawer, calls upstairs to his daughters. Thinking of Sev, he feels it in his belly. He feels guilty, but doesn't know towards whom; he's an adulterer, but his wife isn't his wife anymore. He doesn't get how Sev can be so different, so close and yet so far, so terribly different, from him, from Terri. *Not a relationship, just this island in time.* Her words. Lovers. He arranges the cheese between the slices of tomato.

"What are we having?" Ally sits down. Her skinny shoulders poke out of her shirt. The smooth curtain of hair conceals most of her face.

"Pasta. Where's your sister?" He sets a full plate in front of her and a less full plate across from her, at Krista's place. He starts tearing basil leaves for the salad.

"I'm not hungry," Krista says before she's reached the bottom of the stairs.

"There," Ally says, pointing at her sister without looking up.

"What do you mean, there?"

"She is."

"She?"

Krista tosses her phone into the basket on the dresser—one of Terri's rules—and sits down, arms crossed. David sets a plate for himself on the table, a glass, water for the kids.

"I'm not hungry," Krista repeats, staring at her shrimp with an expression that looks more like anger than anything else. Bad timing, he thinks. It is now, just as they're starting to detach from him, to establish their own identities opposed to their parents', that he needs them, like a drowning man clinging to his piece of wreckage. No going back, there's no going back. If only they were little again, if only Terri were still here, he might have been in time to swing the wheel about, no idea when, no idea where to, all that time he'd thought they were sailing a true course —to keep that silly metaphor going. He tries to ignore the scowling face of his oldest child. Ally slurps up a piece of spaghetti.

"Yummy, Daddy."

"Great, kiddo."

"May I be excused?" Krista shoots him a pained look.

"No."

"The smell makes me sick."

"I just want you to take a bite."

"Because?"

"I haven't cooked a whole dinner for nothing."

"Did I ask you to?"

"You can't not eat."

"Why not?"

"You'll die." Ally says it in all seriousness.

Krista nibbles on a minuscule piece of parsley. She's thinking about Rafik's bare brown arms. His skin gleams, maybe he rubs it with oil; she thinks of the sign in the window of the shop with exotic wares, *Moroccan soap, liquid gold*. Rafik's eyes. The hair at Rafik's neck. She'd give anything to know what he's thinking, she's sure everything he thinks is brilliant. Maybe she wouldn't get it. But she's sure he has lots of thoughts, awesome thoughts, and lots of feelings, deep feelings, not as banal as her own. She thinks of the way he danced, the djellaba whirling around his legs. She thinks about his mouth, his lips, and her lips. The way he would kiss her. Don't think about it, not now, later, when she's alone and can give herself over to it, not here with her dad and her sister, who with their presence un-purify—if that's a word— her thoughts. She smells the shrimp, she smells her dad's sweat, she stares at the strands of pasta slick with oil on her plate.

Ever since her mother walked out on them, her life's become more interesting in the eyes of others. Not in his eyes, or maybe in his eyes as well. He looks at her, but she's got no idea what he sees. His eyes, his eyes. Stop, don't go there, not now. Ally and David have polished off their plates. There's grease on her dad's chin. Her mother left them. In a conversation she wasn't supposed to over-hear, her mom told him he *disgusted* her. Ally refused to believe it when Krista told her, but she cried anyway. Ally's still a little kid, she only wants it to get better, she has no idea that the marriage, a marriage, a marriage like the one her parents had, isn't anything worth having. You'd just die of boredom. Her dad has no idea how disgusted he'd be with Terri, if he knew what Krista knows.

"Can I sleep over at Tirza's tomorrow?"

"Can't Tirza come and sleep here?" He and Terri often used to talk about it, about how easy it is to pick them out, the children from broken families, about the exceptions only proving the rule. About Tirza who is far too precocious, who smokes and drinks and hides behind that blank expression of hers.

David doesn't think they ever disagreed there. With Sev, everything's different. She has been trying to show him a different perspective, her circle of friends is rife with nontraditional families and amicable divorces. But that only makes him more depressed, as do the examples she gives, he is such a believer in marriage, he's always believed in it heart and soul, he can't imagine how children can feel at home in more than one place, how you can raise kids without being a couple, how love can work outside the tie that binds. He can't imagine how, once his job of delivering the kids to adulthood is done, his life could be anything other than a yawning abyss.

"Why can't I sleep over at her house?"

"I'm not saying you can't."

"So then I can?"

"I'd rather she came here."

"Whyyyyy?" Drawn out, a word implying petulance rather than wonder.

Krista doesn't smoke, he is certain of that. And she doesn't drink either, he's certain of that too. He needs to be extra strict. He wants to be extra nice. How can someone be a good mother, and then suddenly, from one day to the next, just call it quits? What did he miss?

"I don't trust her."

"You don't trust *me*."

"I don't trust *her*."

"If you don't let me sleep over at her house, you don't trust me."

"I do trust you."

Just before Terri left for good, left him, left all three of them, she had begun to weave a new vocabulary into their exchanges: "honesty," for example, suddenly became "sincerity." That's how he knew the words weren't hers. That they were *his*.

"Well? So?"

"What?"

"Dad!"

"Yes!"

"We're not going out."

"What are you going to do, then?"

"Just—nothing."

"What's nothing?"

"I don't know. Nothing. Chillin'. Talking. Netflixin'."

"No smoking."

"Okay."

"No drinking."

"Okay." How easy it is to reassure him. How childish they are, parents.

David clears the dishes. Ally stacks them in the dishwasher. He pours what's left of the bottle into his glass. That bottle was full this afternoon. A year ago, or maybe two, Terri decided there would be no more drinking on weekdays. It wasn't a suggestion, and it wasn't meant only to apply to herself. He hadn't been consulted on that ruling; it was just suddenly a given, referred to as a fact set in stone. *No, it's Wednesday*, she'd say if he asked if she'd like a glass of wine, so that he'd think, *Oh, that's right, it's Wednesday*, and then he wouldn't have one either, he'd just glug down a glass of water at the sink, as if to persuade himself it was thirst that had prompted the suggestion. Why didn't he ever protest, why didn't he view it as a problem, never even gave it a second thought, resigning himself to tossing back the occasional glass of wine in the kitchen on the sly, or stopping at a café for a beer on the way home? On the sly. How come those concessions only strike him as strange now? How can he explain to Sev how that works, how it worked, who he was back then—who he may still be, except that he feels lost, floundering in an overabundance of freedom.

He takes the container of vanilla pudding from the fridge, surely she'll have some of that, with chocolate sprinkles ...

"Krista!" She raises her head, excruciatingly slowly. She gazes up at him.

"Yes?"

"Did you finish the pudding?" The container's empty, returned to the fridge empty.

"Yeah."

"Why?"

"There wasn't anything to eat!"

"What do you mean there wasn't anything?"

"Jesus, how can I mean anything different than what I just said?" Those eyes, that slow tilt of the head, that stark impassivity. He wants to shout at her. That he does everything for her, dammit! That she used to be such a sweet little kid! "I'm going upstairs." He holds his tongue, he lets her go, he watches her leave, her lanky body, half child and half ... yes, what, in fact? He shakes a few last drops from the bottle.

"I don't want any dessert." Ally brushes his cheek with a butterfly peck and then she too is gone. Not even twenty minutes after coming downstairs, they're back in their rooms. He runs his finger along the rim of the pan, licks it, then switches on the espresso machine. An argument about that appliance flashes through his mind. Don't do it. Don't rehash everything, like an idiot, that parade of daily scraps that constitutes a marriage. He takes his phone from the basket—he automatically left it there, one of the thousand habits he'll never be able to break.

Three messages. He only reads the one from Sev. He's going there tomorrow evening, to her small apartment with the magnificent views. She'll pour him a glass of wine. She'll tell him to lie down on the bed. She'll undress, the disrobing no more sensual than the act itself. She is voracious. She does things Terri never did. First he'll drown in a flood of shame, then bask in his momentary good fortune. Tomorrow.

"Daddy?" He feels guilty, caught out.

"Ally?"

"I'm going to Isabel's for a bit."

She takes her racket. She shuts the door behind her. Following the narrow strip of shade along the houses, she hops across the pinkish-white markings on the sidewalk. It's hot, it's been hot so long it seems like it'll never end. They're not allowed to go swimming in the canal near their house because of the toxic algae. They're not going on vacation because of the "situation." It's the weirdest summer she's ever had. She bounces the tennis racket on her left knee every other step. If you glued all the hours she's been bouncing balls off the blank school wall end to end, you'd have a week's worth of uninterrupted tennis. She tries to picture it. You'd have to have a ball that lights up in the dark, maybe with fluorescent paint, but there still might not be light enough to see at night, or maybe all the glow would get rubbed off anyway. Isabel and Ally used to try to figure out all kinds of things like that, like, how many hours they'd spent together, or how many minutes they'd been alive up to then—a weird, moving kind of target, since as they were working it out it was already changing.

These days, Isabel isn't interested anymore, she doesn't want to play tennis or work stuff out anymore, all she wants to do is talk. But Ally doesn't know what to say, it's usually about boys, or about the actors on *Oasis Park*, but Ally can't tell them apart because she doesn't watch very often, since she doesn't get what's so great about it. At school Isabel usually acts as if Ally doesn't exist. Out here in the street or on the playground they're constantly disappointing each other. She thinks about before, about a purple blouse of Mommy's that felt so soft against your cheek as you lay curled in her lap, she can hardly believe that that was really her, Ally, lying there, that she was really just three feet tall then, the mark on the wall next to the living room door proves it, five-year-old Ally, three feet exactly. When Terri announced she was leaving because she was suffocating, when she said that, when Ally decided she wasn't going to call her Mommy anymore, her mother was standing right next to that mark, next to five-year-old Ally's mark on the wall. That was me, once, I was there, I once filled the space up to that line, she thought. How do you hold on to a memory that's just a feeling? It's like catching a bird; once you've caught it, you can inspect it up close, but it can no longer do the stuff that makes it a bird. How much she and her mother used to belong together is embodied in the purple silkiness of that blouse. Since Terri is no longer here, she's suddenly having to think not only about her mom but also about her dad—her dad secretly crying in the kitchen. She walks past Isabel's house, to the playground of her old school. At least she can still call *him* Daddy. She lets him console her because it makes him feel better too. On the knee wall opposite are the boys who always seem to be sitting there. Moroccans, says Krista, Afghans, says Isabel. All Ally knows is that those countries aren't particularly close to each other on the map. Stashing two tennis balls on the ground by her feet, she hits a third against the wall. Overhead, underhand, one bounce, no bounce. Her ponytail dances along against her back.

Back at their house around the corner, David mops the floor, brooding about Kahneman's peak–end rule, the theory that says you can't have an accurate grasp of a stage in your life, such as a marriage, because of the impact its ending has on your feelings about it. One floor above him, Krista, using the hall mirror and the one on the inside of her closet door, inspects her backside.

On the other side of the river, in the spartan interior of the rental apartment on the same street where she lived as a college student, Terri is shaving her legs. She is fond of this ritual form of getting ready, she has nice legs, smooth skin. She trims her pubic hair into a neat triangle. This afternoon she started on the second letter to Krista, the letter that will be the final blow, but she doesn't know that yet—for the moment she still thinks it's a good move to give her fifteen-year-old daughter a full explanation. She is still incapable of seeing what a shambles she's made of it, and doesn't realize that everything she does to improve the situation is just more fuel on the fire. It's only a matter of time, she thinks, a matter of time until everything settles into something new, something calm and peaceful, a life the way she's imagined it, the way thousands of people are able to make it work. Divorced, but amicably, a bit the worse for wear, but alive; retaining the love for the children, caring for them as before, only untethered from the family, a single person again. Responsible, but free. She rubs oil into her legs, vitamin E cream for the stomach and breasts, another cream for her face and throat, something else again on lips and eyelids; she's spent a fortune on these little jars, she never allowed herself the indulgence before.

Sometimes she'll be gripped with the fear that it's all a mistake, and a memory will spring up out of nowhere, David at twenty-five, at thirty, how head over heels in love she was, although—who, *she*? The Terri she was then is very far away; how can you remember your younger self except as a hazy dream? As soon as she tries to zoom in on that self, it dissolves. The way she overcomes the moments of doubt is by focusing on the person she is now, on the body she's in now, on the longings that have become her guide. Or she'll zero in, briefly but harshly, on David at forty-nine, who's scared of everything, who stepped down from his management position, who gets claustrophobic in traffic jams, who falls asleep on the couch after dinner, who's been wearing the same style of pants and telling the same jokes for twenty-five years. When she focuses on those things, the feeling she's made a mistake evaporates; she remembers the burden that was lifted when she left David. Then her thoughts drift seamlessly to Lucas, who is about to arrive, who is "the cause of all the misery" according to David, by which he means only his own misery. Lucas was just the catalyst. David screamed when she used that word.

He, the catalyst, is picking up his suits from the dry cleaner's; he doesn't know about the screaming, he wouldn't like it, not because it was about him, but simply because he finds people who scream unappealing. Many of the things most people believe in are of no consequence at all to Lucas: stormy emotions, romantic love, marriage, equality, nonviolence, democracy. When he arrives home he takes the stairs two at a time, hangs up the dry cleaning, shuts the closet door with an underhand swing that gives him the momentum for a perfect 360-degree spin on his heel. Vigorous, that's how he feels. He glances in the mirror, is satisfied with his square-jawed, handsome face; he seldom thinks back to when he was a chubby kid and something of a misfit. He doesn't know about Terri and David's fights, but he could imagine what they're like. He could, but he doesn't. It's bad enough that she's got an entire family trailing in her wake, an angry husband, two angry daughters, joint bank accounts and debts, the whole hodgepodge of conjugal goods. He wants nothing to do with that legacy. He goes downstairs again, to his kitchen flooded with sunlight, a kitchen seldom used for cooking, he thinks about Terri and feels his body responding, there's something savage about her, something greedy, something that won't relax, he finds it very attractive.

This morning he went to see a prostitute, he won't tell Terri about it, he doesn't believe in total candor either. In a hypothetical discussion, he would say to her, That's exactly why your marriage failed, it's taken you twenty-five years to realize that reciprocal ownership, having a say over each other's lives, sexual tastes, and fantasies, is the kiss of death. If you sacrifice yourself, there's nothing left of you in the end. But Terri wouldn't know how to accept the discussion for what it was, just a discussion; she'd only hear the bit about sacrificing herself, she'd be worried she couldn't trust Lucas, and in that desolate no-man's-land between the two, between togetherness and being alone, she wouldn't know what to say. He drinks a glass of water. What's so easy about whores is that you pay for what you want and then just walk out the door, no obligations. He doesn't go for women who are visibly addicted, or sick, or too cheap. They appreciate his business, he believes; he is clean and handsome and well behaved. He always goes for the same thing, a blowjob and a fuck, preferably anal. And when, reinvigorated, he walks out the door, he feels like a prince.

That night the city barely cools off. David stares wide-eyed into the dark of his bedroom, he's thinking about all that has to get done, about all that's resting on his shoulders, about the family therapist who's put them on a waiting list, about the futility of his anger about that, anger that isn't going to get things moving any faster. Just as his thoughts start to drift from all the tasks awaiting him to the next day, when he's planning to leave work early, four o'clock if he's lucky, and spend an extra long time at Sev's, past midnight (a party, is the fib he'll tell his children); just as he's mentally seeing himself with her, with her creamy body and sharp mind, with the wonderful sensation of finally being his true self, although that self is someone he barely knows, he is startled by a scream. Ally: his vigilance called for again. Nightmares, he adds to his list of worries. After peeking in at her sleeping face, carefully shutting the door again and padding back to the top floor, where it's hotter than hell, and laying his sweaty body back down under the sheet, he goes over the whole list again: Ally's nightmares, Krista's schoolwork, her refusal to speak to Terri, the divorce still to be finalized, alimony, mortgage, custody arrangement, Christmas, vacations, her parents—how is *that* supposed to work, is it her responsibility from now on to ensure the children see their grandparents?— the therapist, persuading Terri to remain open to it while they're on the waiting list. A therapist, she'd asked, what do you expect to come of it? Peace, he'd said. And she'd given him a dirty look. He wishes she were dead, he lies in bed with his hands balled into fists, he wishes she were dead and he a widower.

Terri, across the river, tries to relax, starting at her toes and then moving up, it's her own body she should be focusing on, not Lucas's body breathing beside her, a body she wants to feel on top of hers again, she's got the feeling the weight of his body is the only thing that will calm her down. Lucas has drunk what for him is a great deal of wine, and is breathing heavily. In his drowsy state his thoughts wander to tomorrow morning, when on waking up, he'll fuck her again; he wonders if she'll let him do whatever he wants, he thinks about her small, firm ass.

Ally dreams she's swept up in a crowd and has lost the others, she's being jostled along by the panic of strangers, she trips and falls and someone tramples her underfoot.

Krista wakes up, it could have been Ally's scream, although she doesn't know that, and puts her hands between her legs. She thinks about Rafik with a vague sense of guilt, as if she could be blowing her chances this way. Until recently she never thought about boys when she did it, it was always a purely physical sensation, nothing to do with anyone else; now that it's turned into something tied to love and desire, she thinks she's discovered something important.

Sev is alone; she stayed up working until half past one. She wishes she had David lying in bed beside her, but her fantasy falters when she tries to imagine what a future with him would look like. She thinks about the other men she's lived with, Felix and later Johan, she thinks about Ernst and about the time he lived here with Hendrik and her. She would often lie in bed awake, brooding that now she'd have to sleep next to him for the rest of her life. Then she'd get out of bed, tiptoe out of the bedroom and go read or work in the kitchen until Hendrik woke up for his bottle. When Ernst was at the office and Hendrik at day care, she would sleep. By the time they split up and he left, she was exhausted, disappointed in herself too; she had lost, although a little voice inside her said she just hadn't had the right opponent. Ernst said it was Hendrik he felt most sorry for; Sev retorted that children aren't born with bourgeois ideals. Ernst said that for him it wasn't about the bourgeois ideal but the romantic ideal. Sev said romance was a Hollywood concept, upon which Ernst looked at her with such pity and sorrow. You'd be surprised how romantic I am, Sev thought, but she didn't say it because she didn't know if it was true.

Since Hendrik was born, she has found herself surrounded by families. She observes them in an attempt to disprove Tolstoy's famous line. She started off assuming it to be true. And if it's true that all happy families are alike, she thought, then it stands to reason there must be a formula, or some secret ingredient, that all happy families have in common. Starting from that premise, she decided she only had to get to know two happy families well in order to discover the secret. She wondered if being happy means your desires conform with reality, or that you're just always in a good mood, or if happiness is largely an irrational state of mind brooking neither doubt nor objection. And then she realized that the combination of "happy" and "family" is in itself rather problematic. Can a family be a happy one if the individual members of that family are not? Or the reverse? What does family happiness mean, assuming there's more to it than basic circumstances, such as prosperity and good health? Isn't there, rather, some quality in the individual that makes him or her intrinsically suited to finding happiness within the family? By the same token, she could see that unhappiness is similarly consistent: the irritation, the stifling atmosphere, the lack of appreciation and tenderness. She thought: Happiness or unhappiness, they're all the same, all over. Until you look more closely. Maybe Tolstoy couldn't have foreseen that that line of his would become so iconic; you might say it's a rather weak aphorism, but it's so often quoted, whether applicable or not (even outside literature), that it's taken for granted that writing about happy families won't make for a very long book, or a very good book—thus reinforcing the notion that Tolstoy articulated an important truth.

David had a happy family. And for twenty-five years, a good marriage. He calls Terri's departure a disaster. His problem is that he can't get over it, just as Sev's problem is that she has never been able to believe in the happy family. He may be just the research subject she's been looking for.

THE PREVIOUS FALL

Wasted potential

The groceries have been delivered to the kitchen, the chalkboard over the sink displays the week's menu, today is Tuesday, and Terri's enthusiasm-dampening assignment is chicken, green beans, and potatoes, Ally's favorite. When she complains about this system, David says it was her idea, that she's the one who made him put that chalkboard up there. As if you can't be annoyed at your own ideas, but Terri wishes she could tell him it's his fault that she came up with it in the first place. That he is the root cause of her endlessly shrinking world.

Kris and Ally are doing their homework upstairs. She can't tell them to come down and work at the kitchen table, they're long past that stage; their grades may be so-so, but at least they aren't failing and won't have to repeat the year. Krista's unwillingness to do anything more than she absolutely has to drives Terri crazy; there's not an ounce of ambition in the teaching materials, and there's not an ounce of ambition in Krista either.

Putting away the groceries, she reflects on how her body has been stripped of its youthfulness, and how their lives have been drained of any aspiration. Everything's fine, it's all hunky-dory, isn't it? he says. Living together, she thinks to herself, means constantly wading right into the communal pond: shallow, lukewarm, with a sludgy bottom. The only exceptions tolerated are those that benefit the common good. The fact that she isn't particularly bothered by lack of sleep was a blessing when their children were babies, but the fact that she sometimes stays up half the night nowadays somehow makes her a traitor.

She flattens the crates and puts them out in the hall. Lucas thinks she's pretty, not just normal-pretty, but exceptionally pretty, objectively pretty. David has never told her she's beautiful, not once in all these twenty-five years. Every time she was seized by insecurity he would try to comfort her, but not by contradicting her; he'd act all sympathetic, which is as bad as confirming there's a problem. He'd pat her arm, as if to say don't you worry. Lucas makes her see herself in a different light. Maybe she *is* pretty. Maybe that's one of the many aspects of her wasted potential. She walks upstairs, past her daughters' rooms, which face each other: Krista's room is a mess, a lair, a place wallowing in the clichés of puberty, without the slightest urge to excel. Ally's room is still the room of a child, teeming with toys and dolls and crafts, arranged according to Ally's personal concept of order. With Lucas her own putative beauty isn't the only thing they talk about; he is good at showing her that everything she holds to be true is open to question, he challenges her intellectually. He is a nihilist, he says so himself, he accepts nothing at face value and categorically rejects anything that reeks of duty or obligation. Sometimes he doesn't know how to hold back where her life is concerned. He doesn't understand why she insists on hewing to her family when that family is tying her down. He thinks her choice not to deal with the situation is in itself a statement. The only goal in life is self-fulfillment, he says, quoting Wilde or Sartre or someone. Lucas made love to her in a completely selfish way, which in theory she hates, but which in practice gave her an emotional and physical boost. It woke her up, his roughness broke through a wall that had been keeping an entire dimension of her existence out of reach. She goes upstairs, to their ochre bedroom, the bed in which night after night she listens to David breathing, each breath sucking a bit more oxygen from the room, shrinking the space left for her. She changes into her running clothes. She won't tell the girls she's going, they don't care anyway, her running is considered a silly hobby, by David too, although it would be so good for him if he'd follow her example, if he would just *do* something sometime.

He's growing fat around the middle, hard to miss because he is lean by nature, he snores and his erection isn't as hard as it used to be. She should put him on a strict diet. He'd follow it too, he's a man who likes to obey the rules. She pulls her hair back, rubs her knees, bounds down the stairs.

In the front hall, David is taking off his shoes.

"Hey, you're home already?" She remembers her phone, which she left lying on the kitchen table, with Lucas's messages, she's never erased any of them, so that when he doesn't write, she can read the old ones. Just for a moment she hopes David will read them, but David is too decent to do that. He'd only read them if it weren't wrong to do so, if it didn't amount to an invasion of privacy or breach of common decency. She does see the possibility, suddenly, of letting him know that way, of letting him discover her affair by accident, leaving a letter out, her email open, a message that isn't clearly not meant for his eyes, its contents compelling enough that he won't look away once it dawns on him what it means. She ought to tell him. But what should she tell him? It would be an oversimplification, the truth turned into something banal, if he thought she was in love, that she was simply in love with another man.

"Yeah." He gives her an absentminded kiss, and goes into the kitchen.

He is bone-tired. He's good at his job. He is sharp, analytical, he has integrity. He doesn't need to shine, he's your ideal number-two man. His work is appreciated, he sees the results of his efforts, earns a decent salary. He's happy to be home, and he's happy Terri's going out running, so there's no need to summon more energy than he has in him right now. He starts snapping off the tops of the green beans. His mother used to do it with a knife, Terri too does it with a knife; his method, using scissors, is much faster, but it's probably cheating, he thinks. He leaves the beans to soak in cold water and starts scrubbing the potatoes. It's Terri's turn to cook today, but he's giving her a head start. He's longing for a drink. Music wafts down from upstairs. He leans forward, hands on the table, weary, tentative, but also the very image of a man about to raise his head to address the boardroom.

When Terri returns from her run, he's still standing there. Or again. She stares at his socks, his navy pants, the white shirt, the rather messy hair above. She sees that he has prepped the meal, to help her, of course, but to her that only underscores what a ragbag of tasks, what a production unit they are, the well-oiled machine whose smooth operation has become the goal itself. *We have to talk*, says the voice in her head. If only it weren't such a ghastly line, such a hideous cliché to introduce what she wants to say. As if she even knows what she wants to say. Kris has turned her music up loud, too loud, a provocation.

"David."

"Terri."

"I won't be home for dinner."

"What?" He's still standing there with his hands spread wide on the table. "Why not?"

"I have to get … out for a bit."

"Out of where?"

"There's something I've got to do."

"Something you've got to do. What are you talking about? What do you have to do?"

"Something. Different. Something else."

He turns and looks at her, the horizontal groove over his nose at its deepest. She gazes at him. She grabs her foot from behind and stretches her thigh muscle. Standing on one leg like a heron, she stares at her prey, him, ready for the kill.

"You're telling me now?"

"Only just remembered it."

"On your run?"

"Yeah."

A few months ago they took a trip to Berlin without the kids. They had sex, and not in their routine way. They talked, they had real conversations with minimal exchange of practical information, they got drunk, he got her to laugh, they saw beautiful things, they took the time to look—at a building, a painting, a movie, each other. They fell asleep together. They replenished their love. Looking at her mouth now, at her expression, chin raised, confrontational, waiting for the hostile response, there isn't much left of it. What did she say again? That she had something to do, but she didn't say what.

"It's not that you really have to be somewhere else, you just want to get out of here."

"Yes."

Okay, David thinks to himself, that's fine, that ought to be possible. He wants to tell her in a warm, deep voice that it's cool, no need to explain, just go have a nice evening.

"It was your turn to cook," he says with an almost imperceptible tilt of his head at the chalkboard.

"You'll have no problem finishing it by yourself."

It would help if he could tell that she actually enjoyed it, the running, but as far as he can tell it's all drive and discipline with her, and she's usually in a terrible mood when she gets home. Yes, now that he thinks about it, she's always cross when she's been out for a run. As if the effort whips up her slumbering fury into something concrete.

"Are you mad at me?"

After a long pause, and with some hesitation, she says yes. And it isn't the opening of a conversation; there's just a deep chasm between them reverberating with her Yes. When they had just started seeing each other, he had a rival, Richard, a musician, a flamboyant kid, much more exciting than he could ever be, but he and Terri read the same books, and Richard made her feel shy, whereas David brought out her own flamboyant side. She liked the way she was a foil to his respectability, the way David gave her plenty of space, but also the guarantee that he'd be there to pick her up if she fell. She remembers the first night he stayed with her, touched her, torn between desire and excessive caution. That she softly whispered *It's okay*. She reminds herself that for weeks, months, years, he was just right, gentle and strong, funny and earnest. That she got to know him slowly, his history, his way of thinking. That together they embarked on something new. That they cast out the old like snakes shedding their skins, meeting each other halfway, giving it a new gloss, building on the story, building up the family, the project. That they joined destinies, and gave up their independence. That the mystery began to unravel, and ultimately melted into thin air. Such a sense of emptiness those memories give her now, so much so that she only recognizes those earlier feelings from her own stories, or the photo albums. She despises his predictability, his conservatism, his devotion—that special, intense form of devotion, with duty as an essential component, that sense of responsibility of his, which now just fills her with infinite despair. She's still looking at him. He is tired, she can tell. He's always tired. His look a mix of weariness, incomprehension, and distaste.

"Are you having a fight?" Krista has come downstairs without making a sound. The standoff ends. Terri circles her arms back a few times. David looks at her shoulders and her knees. Nice shoulders, nice knees.

"No, we're not having a fight. Right, Terri baby?" Her mother doesn't say anything; she's looking sad. Her father looks at her with a shrug, forging a little bond of perplexity about Mom with her.

"What time are we having dinner?
"In an hour. Homework done?"
"Yeah."
"Okay."

"Okay." She puts on her coat, shuts the front door, and takes a deep breath, her hand clutching the pack of Lucky Strikes in her pocket. It's cold outside, and drizzling rain. She can see herself reflected in the windows. She has a bounce in her step. Maybe she'll be allowed to sleep over at Tirza's on Saturday. Her mother is almost never home. Tirza often eats dinner by herself. Then there's food in the fridge, or her mom will leave money for her on the table. Terri and David say Tirza is a neglected child, but in Krista's view she's free, free of the burden of being the child of responsible parents. When she gets home Tirza never has to say where she's been. Tirza's mother always takes her side when she's in a fight, even if it's a teacher, she always believes Tirza and that's because there's no reason to lie. Tirza even smoked a joint with her mother once.

Where the path up the acoustic wall begins, she sees the Moroccan boys who seem to be swarming all over the neighborhood these days. There's six of them. The only one she really recognizes is the one boy, the rest are interchangeable, but that one is different, quieter, as if his mind is elsewhere, as if he's detached from them, a cut above the rest, destined for something great, just keeping a low profile among the others until then. She takes a minimal step sideways, feels five pairs of eyes ogling her body as she approaches and, once she's passed them, in her back; he's the only one who isn't looking, he's just staring into space. Their leering doesn't embarrass her, Tirza says it's only a problem if they *don't* look at you, and Krista has accepted that as gospel, as she accepts most of the things Tirza says about life. Right now she isn't particularly bothered by those five boys looking at her, what she's really aware of is that *he* isn't looking at her. Tirza is already up there, she's sitting on the bench tapping at her phone.

In the street below is the house, indistinguishable from the other row houses except for the color of the curtains. In the kitchen David leans against the counter waiting for the beans to boil, confused as to what he should be catching hold of for it not to slip through his fingers. Terri, meanwhile, is putting more and more distance between herself and her house. By the time her wheels have completed a hundred revolutions, her guilt has been blown away.

After crossing the long bridge, with the wind in her hair, her coat flying open, with life itself manifested like a promise in the fresh humid air, she hesitates. Should she let him know she's on her way? She doesn't know if he'll like it if she just drops by. It's been exactly a week since he undressed her and made her lie down the way he wanted, gazing at her as an object. It excited her. It excites her. At first, when they were just colleagues working on a project together, and all he did was make her thoughts race, filling her with energy and mental sharpness, when the word love hadn't yet taken shape in her mind, and she'd brought that renewed energy home with her, and it had rubbed off on David as well—the time they'd gone to Berlin for instance, when Lucas hadn't yet wholly taken over her thoughts, but she seemed to be drawing from some new source of energy that had no name, no distinct meaning, but was hers—she'd been happy. She couldn't remember ever having been as happy, as alive. A group of girls step out into the street right in front of her. She swerves to avoid them. She turns into his street and leans her bike against a pole. Light in the windows, the front steps leading up to the door. She rings the bell. She waits. She glances over her shoulder. She hopes he isn't home. She turns to find herself staring into his face. A smile breaks through his frown.

"Terri!"

"What am I doing here?" He takes off her coat, his hand grabs her by the neck, he drags her into his apartment, lets go again. Two connected rooms. His laptop on the dining table. On the olive-green sofa beyond the pocket doors lies an open book, a textbook, judging by its format. His phone goes off. The noise makes time slow down. He stares at her until it stops ringing.

"Wine?" She feels her face grow red. She swallows. She nods. What is she doing here? He narrows his eyes, notices her blushing, doesn't remark on it. It was her cynical humor, her intelligence, her invulnerability that charmed him. He's dragged her out of her comfort zone and now here she is standing in his living room blushing like a schoolgirl. He fills two glasses. He's not sure if he should put into words what she's come for—which would only make her blush worse—ignore it, or simply brush it off. Send her away. He laughs out loud.

"Am I disturbing you?"

"No, why?"

"Were you working?"

"Reading." Not true. He was watching a movie. He hands her a glass.

"Cheers."

"To what?"

"Movement."

"Shouldn't you be home?"

"No." She doesn't feel like explaining.

"Here." He slides a book across the table at her. "I'd like to know what you think of it. Put it in your bag." He looks at her with a mocking gleam in his eyes. "We're not going to talk about work. Are we?" he says.

She doesn't look at the book, leaves it where it is and puts her hand on his chest.

"Although," he says, "but—this isn't about work, strictly speaking—one thing: I spoke with Andrea and I think she knows there's something between us."

Andrea is a student who works with them.

"Is there something between us, then?"

"Isn't there?"

"What is it, then?" She looks amused, but there's something greedy in her gaze as well.

"Must we define it?"

"Well. No. Not as far as I'm concerned."

"No, as far as I'm concerned we needn't either, as far as I am concerned there's no need to give it a name," he says.

"No," she says.

"Unless you want to."

He's twisting it around, didn't he start off calling it "something"? "I wouldn't say there's something between us," she says, trying to sound nonchalant.

"Yet we do have something, don't we?"

"Something?" She kisses him. She has the feeling she's won back some terrain, although the idea of their *something* being a battleground is also alarming.

"Let's just call it something." He puts down his glass and cups his hands over her breasts. He is both more male and more suave than

David, but she doesn't want to compare them, she mustn't compare them.

"But I *am* married."

"Yes."

"That's also quite ... something."

"But being married isn't all that you are. You're also an individual." And in stating the obvious, he is right, of course. Yes, she's also an individual. When did her life as an individual become so inextricably bound up in the need to be held to account? At first it's automatic, that togetherness, that merger, because it matches your desires. You fall for it. But then, later, how do you extricate yourself, and how do you do that without ruining everything? Lucas can't help her there, he isn't married.

"Yes, that's been pushed a bit into the background." He's never lived with anyone. He is a complete amateur in that department. He starts unbuttoning her blouse. She wants to kiss him, but he turns his head away and, by keeping his arms extended and leaning back, increases the distance between them. He opens her blouse and gazes at her breasts. Lovely, he says. Lovely. First he wanted to know if she would cheat on her husband. Now he wants to know if she's prepared to have an affair. If she's capable of starting something with him. If she'll defend her marriage, or if that marriage of hers will lose its luster. He did meet the husband once, David, but that was before his interest in her took this turn, and he can't really remember what he's like. According to Terri, David's a nice guy, which to Lucas seems a deplorable qualification. He does something for the government, mediation or something, reasonableness incarnate. In her there's something wild, something adventurous. He pinches her nipples. It makes him think of an ex-girlfriend. *They aren't knobs*, she'd once cried indignantly, but Terri's are definitely knobs, when he twists them her lips fall apart.

"I don't have much time." Best to put it off, not give in to what she wants, best to send her packing.

"What?"

"We'll have to finish this another time."

"Oh really?" She hides her chagrin in the blink of an eye and recovers her aloof expression, the expression he used to find intimidating. She straightens her underwear and buttons her blouse.

"Sorry." He puts a hand to her cheek; combined with his professorial frown, it's an ambivalent gesture.

"I don't know if there will be another time," she says.

See, he thinks, it's going well.

"I hope there will be."

"Yeah?"

"I'll dream about your body."

She makes an indistinct sound. She picks up the book. *You Must Change Your Life* by Peter Sloterdijk. He leads the way into the hall. At the door they kiss. He whispers in her ear that he likes her. He shuts the door after her. He never read that book. Don't forget that life's a game, every relationship a crapshoot. She's on her way back, back to her suburb, back to her husband, but it's Lucas she'll be thinking about all night. Her short visit has revived him, after he spent all afternoon lethargically binge-watching TV shows on his laptop. He jacks off in the kitchen. He wants to get to the gym before dinner. He likes staying trim, at least there he has a distinct advantage over David, the dutiful bureaucrat; at least that's how Terri tells it, that David's too tired to exercise and that he doesn't enjoy it anyway. He washes his hands and starts whistling something, what is it again? Mozart or something.

Terri pedals back across the endless bridge, slowly now, her legs leaden. He had just poured the wine; did he forget he had somewhere to go, and suddenly remember once he'd already stripped her half-naked? What is she doing? She has a good marriage. Every objective factor confirms it. David is a nice man, he is clever and healthy and tender and devoted and, sure, there is something apathetic about him lately, but is that a reason, isn't everyone entitled to go through a bout of apathy sometime? Time is the sculptor of love, who wrote that? Don't throw away something you've put so much time, so much of yourself into. Yes, he does take it for granted, her, and it, he isn't giving it his all, not the way she would like, he doesn't really listen when she talks about her work, he never seems to do anything new or different, he makes love to her thoughtlessly, he comes too soon. When they'd only just met, they used to go swimming in the IJsselmeer; they'd found a spot where nobody ever came. They feasted on treacle sandwiches, apples, and water, they swam, he said she was the cutest girl he'd ever met, they still used to smoke back then, roll-ups, because they were poor, they smoked and gazed at the clouds. Within three months he had moved in with her. He was energetic and felt responsible for her, for his mother, for his sister, for his own health. He wasn't radical in any way, he possessed a grand sense of justice, was driven by a well-reasoned set of rules, of morals, he always knew the right thing to do, she thought that was great about him. She was in love, and after that she'd simply loved him, and they had a good life, all that time, until suddenly she discovered it was gone; that the place where the love was supposed to dwell was now occupied by a reservoir of secret thoughts. When did that happen? Two years ago perhaps, maybe even longer. Peering into the front window, she sees David cleaning the counter. A man in a house, her spouse. A person. What does he do or think in the part of him that can't be shared? She's afraid he's not thinking anything. That inside him there's only a gray, calmly rippling sea. David is simply content, the children too, in fact, they don't desire anything, they lead an uncritical existence within the status quo. She parks her bike in the rack. David is no longer in the kitchen. She waves at Miriam, the woman next door, who's looking out her window. She's probably thinking, *What's that woman doing lurking outside her own front door?* Miriam inside her own house, the mirror image of theirs, another nuclear family with two kids ... If you zoomed out far enough you wouldn't be able to tell the difference, a whole street of married couples and their offspring, animals with their young, population replacement rate achieved, the human race will endure. She cups her breasts in her hands, feeling what Lucas felt and saw.

"Hi there." In the living room, David and Ally are flopped on the couch watching a show.

"You're back."

"I'm back."

"That didn't take long."

"No."

"Everything okay?"

"No."

"No?"

"No. *Everything*'s not always okay."

"Mom."

"Yes?"

"What's the matter?"

"Nothing. I just think *everything*'s a bit much."

"What do you mean?" Ally is looking at her in alarm and David gives an exaggerated, annoyed, reproachful, petty, tired, old, drained, unattractive, cross, indignant sigh, and inside her sprouts a poisonous arrow she'd like to drive right between his eyes. David gives Ally a kiss and pushes her legs off his lap.

"Be back in a minute, Allybel." And, "Come," addressed to her. He walks back upstairs, to the kitchen, takes out a bottle of red, ignoring her disapproving glare at the bottle.

"Just tell me what's going on, what I've done wrong."

Terri says nothing.

"Where were you just now?"

Terri says nothing.

"Do you still need to eat?"

She won't look at him.

"Are you going to respond in any way?"

Maybe it's his fault. He should take her in his arms.

"Are you in love with someone else?"

Casually, almost as a joke, but from the way Terri stays silent, the way her jaw tenses up, he can tell he's right.

"Really?"

"I'm suffocating." And then she clams up again for a while.

"Listen, Terri, talk to me, I am not your enemy. Explain. Help me here."

Okay, she's in love, maybe she's sleeping with the person, can he guess who it is, is it someone he knows? In a flash he sees himself giving her explicit permission, on condition that she doesn't leave, on condition that it will blow over, on condition that nothing's going to change, on condition that she doesn't wreck everything beyond repair. It's that guy, the philosopher, the one working with her on the project for the ministry, suddenly he's certain of it, he's even met him once or twice, what's his name again, Oscar, no, shit, he can't remember!

"Who is it?"

"That's not the point. It's not about being in love, it's about me suffocating."

"Don't be so cryptic."

"I'm feeling trapped, you're driving me up the wall, I'm terrified this is going to be my life forever."

"So you don't think it's a good life."

"I think it's a good life in theory."

"In theory."

"But in reality I can't stand it anymore."

"Who is it, I asked."

"It's not about being in love."

"Cards on the table."

"That's what I mean. I don't want to have to justify everything."

"You married me."

"I'm also an individual."

"Jesus!"

"What?"

"Pathetic."

"Lucas."

"Ah, the philosopher!"

"Yes."

"The bogus philosopher."

"If that's how you're going to be, we're better off not talking."

Silence. He twists the corkscrew into the cork. She puts on the kettle, demonstratively. Okay, so she just rode her bike over to that Lucas's place, and they made the decision to tell him. In a café, with their foreheads pressed together, or entwined in his bed.

"Did you sleep with him?"

"Yes."

"Just now?"

"No."

"Before."

"Yes."

"Often?"

"No."

"And now?"

"I don't know."

"We *are* going to have to talk about it, somehow or other."

"Yes."

"Individual to individual."

"Perhaps not right now. Perhaps not when

the kids are home and able to hear everything." They never hear anything. Not yet. But she's right. This is not the right time. But what does that mean? That they should wait to have it out? That until then they'll pretend nothing's been said? They used to go swimming in the IJsselmeer. Why is he thinking of that now? She drops a teabag into a glass and pours water over it.

"Is it my fault?" Of course it's his fault.

"David."

"Yes."

"Don't." Is that a reproach, or an attempt to reassure him?

"It seems to me it's a question of some relevance."

"There's no point discussing it if you put it in those terms." She's way beyond this, that much is clear, she's leaving him in the shade. She isn't thinking in terms of guilt. She's thinking in terms of suffocation. She's allowed to say he's driving her up the wall, but he isn't allowed to ask if it's because of him, something he's done, or because of her, something she's doing. Because she is doing something, that's clear, you don't just fall in love, you don't just bail out on a Tuesday evening when it's your turn to cook dinner for your children.

"I'm going back to Ally. I promised we'd watch a show together."

"Go ahead then."

"Unless you want to talk. Unless you want to answer my questions. Unless you do, because if you don't, I should keep my promise." He manages to give the word "promise" a loaded meaning encompassing their wedding vows.

"Yeah, just imagine if you didn't." And with that brutal smackdown, she manages to ridicule both promises, to dismiss them as silly rituals. The dishwasher cheeps.

"Maybe tonight, later, when the girls are asleep."

"What then?"

"Maybe we can talk then. As long as we don't raise our voices, there's nothing wrong with talking while they're home."

"I don't intend to raise my voice."

"I'll do my best as well."

"I won't talk with you if you're going to start yelling."

"As if I ever yell at you!"

"You just said you'd do your best. That sounds as if what you'd really like to do is yell at me." He turns away. "As if you're having to control yourself!" Now she's the one yelling. He walks away. The bottle remains unopened. He takes the stairs down to the living room, to the big comfy couch, to the television, to his earnest little Ally. He settles back into his usual spot and picks up her legs. He caresses her shins. He takes her soft little feet in his hands. She tries to explain what's happened since he left, they've found a second corpse, but she can't follow the action and explain it to him at the same time, and he doesn't really care, he says. Another time when her parents were having a fight, Mommy said to her, "You get into fights with your friends too sometimes, don't you? It's no big deal, we'll make up again, don't worry, we aren't getting divorced," and as proof they'd hugged, right in the middle of their fight, and waited for her to leave before continuing. That only made it even scarier; yes, she did get into fights sometimes, but those were completely different. On the TV, the cops ring the doorbell of the murdered girl's parents. She hears her dad groaning softly. She wiggles her feet to remind him to press his thumbs into her soles, which he proceeds to do. Tomorrow there's school, but Friday is a half day so she can go play tennis afterwards, or just go play. You're not supposed to play any more when you're in seventh grade, that's the unwritten rule, you're not supposed to want to play, you're supposed to be somebody's fan, you're supposed to have a crush on somebody, you're allowed to get good grades but you're not supposed to let on that you care, you're definitely not supposed to play with boys, and whatever you do, you mustn't show any interest in the immature boys, boys like Bobby and Leo, when Bobby and Leo are the only people (because boys are people too) she can have fun with. Who cares, then just let her be *a recluse*, as Krista calls it. She'd rather be a recluse than in the wrong zoo—not the most perfect analogy, true, because what's the wrong zoo, for Pete's sake, but it does give her a good feeling, and that's where realism ends and poetry begins, her teacher Mr. Eedens would say.

Terri is the only woman David has ever been to bed with, although Terri doesn't know that. When he still lived at home, caring for his mother stopped him from having a girlfriend; he thought it would make her even more depressed, and that it would stand in the way of his duty. The way he was raised made it unthinkable to have sex with someone unless you had serious intentions. Flora, his homework buddy, the girl he used to have deep as well as superficial conversations with, and whom he may have been in love with, and whom he fantasized about screwing almost every night of his senior year, kissed him one night in her bedroom. She was still living with her parents, as was he. It was summer. They were stretched out on her bed talking about what they were going to study at university. She was planning to major in French and he wasn't sure, he was considering taking a gap year, and then, no idea, law maybe, or history. And so although he fantasized about her every night, about watching her take her clothes off, about taking his clothes off himself, about touching her skin, her boobs, her butt, her legs, between her legs, himself between her legs, on top of her, inside her—he never seemed able to think about doing so when he was with her. When he was with her, they were platonic pals, and it wasn't until he was in his own room that she would turn back into a girl, and he'd undress her. She'd suddenly turned around, suspending her face right above his. Her brown eyes shone and she brought her face so close to his that her freckles went out of focus, and then she let her lips land, very soft but resolute, on his mouth. Nothing else happened for a while, and then she flicked his upper lip with her tongue, upon which she was still again for what seemed like an eternity, and then she licked him again, and then she kissed him. He gave her a quick peck in return, they started making out the way he'd imagined it, lips, tongues, warm mouths, harpoon-jolts from his mouth to his crotch, but then he was seized with a panicked sense of duty. He squirmed out from underneath her, stammered an excuse, and fled. It was the end of their intimacy. She did go and study French, but not in Amsterdam, and they lost contact.

By the time David left home to spend four months in the US, his mother's needs no longer dominating his system or routine, with nothing stopping him from having a relationship, serious intentions or not, he was afraid to try. He was twenty-one and still a virgin; that fact alone was embarrassing. Then he turned twenty-two, twenty-three, still a virgin, and by the time he graduated and met Terri, he was twenty-four and still a virgin. He had made out with a girl just one time, for thirty seconds. For Terri, besides exaggerating the business with Flora, he invented an American girl he'd supposedly dated, implying there had been other, more casual hookups. But he never regretted not having racked up more sexual experience; he loved Terri, and the familiarity invariably associated with a long marriage never cramped his excitement. He was sorry they didn't experiment more, that in twenty-five years they never departed significantly from the repertoire established in the first couple of months, he was sorry that it never came up in conversation, that when once he had suggested something, some kind of role-play, she gave him such a pitying look that he felt he'd made a complete fool of himself. He resigned himself to the way things were, he did fantasize about other women, but carefully monitored his daydreams to make sure they were sufficiently abstract; he didn't mind that his choice ruled out the other possibilities, all of it was preferable to the horrifying thought of betrayal, of a secret, of a messy life.

He's uncorked the bottle after all. It's a pleasant, light-red wine, a nice little weekday wine, he thought to himself as he poured himself a glass, and one for her too. Terri is sitting opposite him, her chin resting on her fist. So she's in love with that guy, and she feels suffocated by David, and by the family. She says everything's so terribly static, that he's too set in his ways. The examples she gives flummox him: he doesn't want to learn Italian, he doesn't want to go skydiving, and he doesn't want a vacation in the tropics. She says he is scared and an old stick in the mud. He says he isn't stopping her from doing any of it, and asks why she even wants him to go skydiving with her, for fuck's sake; if she's feeling trapped and wants to be free, isn't it the whole point that he shouldn't come along? She's been reeling them off, the adventures he's supposedly stopping her from having, but in reality what she's doing, the adventure she's now found for herself, is jumping into bed with a guy she works with.

"That story just doesn't hack it, Terri."

"It isn't a story, it's a feeling."

"As if I ever forbid you from doing anything!"

"You just don't understand."

"No, I don't."

"It's not that you're actively telling me. That's not it. It's that our life makes it impossible for me. That your lack of energy is sapping me of my zest for life."

"My lack of energy?"

"Yes!"

"I don't lack energy."

"After dinner you always collapse on the couch and watch TV."

"That's what I enjoy! Besides, I also read—the paper, books, your articles, the kids' homework."

"You've been working on building that fucking chest of drawers for at least ten weekends."

"I enjoy doing that!"

"Ten weeks!"

"It's a project. It's more than just getting it finished. It gives me pleasure."

"You're exhausted."

"Sometimes."

"All the time!"

"I work forty hours a week." She makes a dismissive gesture, as if it's nothing, forty hours. On top of taking care of the children, the house, birthdays, cocktail parties, family, dinners. "And why, for cripes' sake, do you want to go skydiving anyway?"

"See, that's what I mean!"

"What do you mean?"

"You refuse even to consider it!"

"I'm not refusing to consider it, I just can't see it, for me. But that doesn't have to stop you, does it? Aren't you allowed to do whatever you want?"

"Allowed to?"

"Yes. Or able to."

"You don't get it!"

"No!"

"I can't explain it to you, apparently. A fish doesn't know what water is."

"Sorry?"

"I mean you can't see it if you're in it!"

"Jesus, Terri ..."

And then they're silent again. He gets up and draws the curtains. He has to give her space. He's prepared to give her space.

"I want to give you space."

"Is that so?"

"Yes, it is. But I don't want you blaming me for not responding to something I was never asked about. I wasn't aware that I was suffocating you. I thought we had a good life. I'm prepared to listen, I'm prepared to give you space, space for an affair with that guy if need be, but then you have to be open with me, we have to figure out how it's going to work, it's important to be on the same page."

"So you're giving me permission to have an affair."

He nods. On condition that she doesn't leave, that it eventually comes to an end, that she doesn't wreck anything, that they remain a family, that they remain a family unit with

Ally and Krista, and that she gives him a chance to get back in her good graces. An affair, of finite duration, one that gives her a temporary lift, but has her land back in his arms when it's over. But he doesn't say all that.

"How do you see this working, then?"

"Is it the excitement? Is it the thrill of something new, or is it him, as a human being?" She shifts in her chair. "Is it very different, then, with him? Do you do different things with him?" Terri has always refused to give him blowjobs. She said that no woman does it for her own pleasure, that it's a porn myth. "Is he better at it than me?" All self-torture, he knows full well, but he can't seem to stop. "Or is it because of his philosophical ideas? If you had to choose, is it more for his prick, or more for his philosophical ideas?" Rewind, he needs to rewind back to the moment when he said he was willing to give her space, when a tinge of softness, a flicker of startled interest, came into her eyes. "Sorry."

"David."

"Terri."

"I love you." The phrase can be the expression of a feeling, a feeling welling up inside you, wanting to be put into words; it can be the confirmation of a relationship, an endorsement; or it can be a kind of mantra, a mantra of doom, and the latter is what this is. It's a phrase that, in being uttered, tries to evoke the corresponding feeling, but nothing is evoked in her; it's the coldest, deadest, most loveless phrase that exists.

"I love you too." He says it in a sentimental, plaintive voice. "Sorry about that. Sorry. I meant it. I want to give you space."

Maybe it would be better if he didn't, she thinks, maybe it would be better if he threw her out in a rage. Maybe then she could feel that his *I love you* really meant something, whereas now it rings just as hollow as her own. He said she could have an affair, if need be. Is that a solution? It's unexpectedly magnanimous of him, though she expects he doesn't seriously mean it. And she might have seen it coming, the spineless, overeager accommodation, the reasonableness, the fear of letting her down and losing her that way. What would happen if he said, Get out then, and don't come back until you're over it, don't come back until you're ready to choose *me*. What would happen if he fought for her like a knight on a white horse? Her phone chirps. Lucas. She's given him his own ringtone. David pours himself another glass. Alcohol isn't only bad for your health, it's also bad for your emotional life, it numbs you, it lulls you; ever since she realized that and stopped drinking except for some specific reason, a special occasion, she's felt so much sharper, she can see so much more clearly what's wrong with their life.

"But I'm not sure how to go about it right now. What do *you* want?" David stares at her.

"Hmm. What do I want." She wants to look at her phone to see what Lucas has texted her.

"Or maybe we should go talk with some-one."

"What? Why?"

"To find out how to handle it."

"A marriage counselor, you mean?"

"To figure out why you've fallen in love with someone else."

"I don't think I need a marriage counselor for that."

"Tell me."

"I can't."

"Why can't you!"

"I don't want to hurt you."

He stares at her openmouthed, by all indications unaware of his goofy expression. While talking, she's been inching back towards the dresser, and now she snatches the phone from the basket and with one swipe opens the message. *I want to finish what we just started.*

"You don't want to hurt me?"

"No."

"You want to betray me by going to bed with him, but hurting me by telling me why is taking it too far?"

"Right. Tell me I'm being ridiculous." She could make the fight escalate, so she could then storm out the door and cycle back to Lucas's apartment. To finish what they started.

"You *are* being ridiculous. You're being illogical, anyway."

"I'm sorry that my feelings are illogical. In your eyes."

"I'm talking about a fact: infidelity, and

the way you're dealing with it. Your refusal to explain to me something you obviously know perfectly well, I'm not talking about feelings."

"Jesus, David."

"Jesus, Terri."

"Stop acting like a whipped dog."

"Do you really mean that?"

"Yes. Sorry. It's so unattractive." That's mean. And true. Which is more important? He's asking for the truth. She wants to spare him the truth. She doesn't want to tell him how much she loathes him right now. He probably can't help it anyway, his attractiveness has worn off within *her*, not in him. How do you explain that? How do you explain that the feelings you have for each other only exist inside you, and that those feelings can suddenly come to a crashing end even if the other person hasn't changed in any salient way? Hurting him may help, it may push him to stick up for himself for once, so that he'll be angry instead of injured, angry enough to make him hate her, angry enough to show her the door so that she can leave. Lucas. She thinks of his hands on her breasts, the way he pushed her legs apart, grabbed her butt. To David she used to say, You don't make love *to* someone, you make love *with* someone; but Lucas didn't make love to or with her, he simply fucked her, there's no other way of putting it. And suddenly she's sure that it can't be salvaged, David and her.

"Do you want me to go?"

"To him? No."

"That's not what I meant. I meant do you mind my being here?"

"You're confusing things, Terri. *You're* the one who minds. *I* don't mind. I'm not the one feeling suffocated."

"But you are feeling screwed."

"I want us to work things out."

"I don't know if we can."

"You could promise to give it a try, you could promise me that much at least."

"Yes."

"We may not make it, but we owe it to ourselves to do our best to work it out."

"Yes," she says.

"And we owe it to the kids."

"Yes."

"Yes? You think so too?"

"I should go to bed."

"So you don't agree?"

"Yes. I agree."

"You don't sound very convinced."

"But I've said it, haven't I?"

She suddenly seems such a stranger to him, such a strange, hard woman, the way she sits there with her sculpted, muscular body and her stern mouth. Is this his wife? Is this the girl of his youth, with an entire shared life between then and now? Without his noticing she's gone and fallen in love with someone else, while still sleeping beside him, still looking after the children with him, having sex with him as recently as last week—he tries to remember if there was anything different about it. While they were living their lives as if nothing was the matter, she was ditching him right under his nose.

"Is it okay with you if I just go to bed?"

"Yes, of course."

"Do you mind sleeping on the sofa?"

"I do mind."

"Should I sleep on the sofa then?"

"I'd rather you slept in the bed with me. You slept in the bed with me yesterday, didn't you?"

"But it's different now, isn't it?"

"When you slept beside me yesterday, you'd already slept with him, hadn't you?" She sighs and lowers her head in her hands.

"Sorry," he says.

"What are you sorry for?"

"For suffocating you."

She sighs again.

"For robbing you of your zest for life."

"David."

"I'll change. I'll try to change." A whipped dog, he knows.

"Okay, then let's just go to bed."

"Together?"

"Yes. Together."

She goes upstairs and side by side they brush their teeth, although standing beside her he barely dares move. He listens to the sound of the toothbrush scrubbing her molars. She washes her face. Their eyes meet in the mirror.

"David."

"Yes?"

"Sorry."

"What?"

"I've got to go, I just have to … get some air."

"Get some air?"

"Yeah, something like that."

"Something like that."

"I'm …"

"Suffocating."

"Yes."

When she's left the bathroom he sits down on the toilet to pee, his head in his hands. He hears the front door shut. He hears her bike squeaking. Panic swells in his throat. Gone. He has lost her. He tries to breathe, to count to ten, he stares at his hands, are those his hands, he stares at the tiles on the bathroom floor, and then he starts to cry, wildly, out of control, he pulls a towel off the radiator and presses it to his mouth to stifle the noise. He hiccups and weeps and growls, his pants pooled at his ankles. He thinks about his mother weeping in her bed; the way he remembers it, she spent his entire teenage years crying in bed, whereas to the best of his recollection he never cried himself, he can't even remember the last time he cried. And there's deep pity for himself: here he is, always done his best, always done the right thing. He bites into the towel. It's a lonely road, crying in secret, when there's nobody who knows, when there's nobody to console you, until you stop out of pure exhaustion. He stays sitting on that toilet for as long as an hour; then finally he stands up and pulls up his pants, just as Terri, across the river, in Lucas's bedroom, is pulling her pants up and over her hips. Once she's dressed, she stuffs her bra into her coat pocket, bids Lucas goodbye, and walks out the door. Then she gets on her bike to return to her prison.

Quietly she climbs the stairs, undresses and lies down beside him with her back to him. Both lie there wide awake. He smells her: he smells fresh outdoor air and he smells her body, he wants to slide her nightie up and feel her skin against his chest and stomach. He wants to wrap his arms around her, wants to hold her, her body that belongs to him, that belongs to their marriage, the body she's supposed to share with him, the body that has changed over the course of twenty-five years, that was once plumper, skinnier, that once was young, that was pregnant, that's been sick, that's grown more and more streamlined in the past few years—something he doesn't find particularly attractive, it may be beautiful, but her chubbiness felt nicer, the body she has now is largely a feat of willpower. Her body, which, even with those changes, was always a constant, a constant factor in his life, a constant presence. He feels tears welling up in his eyes again.

"David?"

"Yes?" It could also turn out all right, married couples do survive crushes, crises, periods of separation, doubts, skydiving.

"Do you mind not breathing so noisily?"

A lover

On the floor behind her a Lego battle is in full swing. Hendrik, sprawled on his stomach, is directing the troop movements. He employs different voices, sings wordless battle hymns, bellows and shouts on behalf of his soldiers on the ground. It's raining a bit, the river is as gray as the sky above. Sev is looking at her phone, swiping through the men selected for her on the basis of her preferences. The degree to which she may be a good fit for a particular candidate is expressed in numbers. The highest score goes to an executive with three kids who believes in possibilities and hasn't lived if he hasn't laughed that day. What he can't live without is coffee, and oxygen, and he'd like to meet Barack Obama in person. Sev thinks for Obama that might be a waste of time. And for her too. Why is the algorithm choosing men like that for her? What kind of lame-brained answers did she give herself? She has begun exchanging messages with two of the men. One is a lawyer, the other a manager. She doesn't know what sort of man she's looking for, if it matters what sort of thing the managers manage, what sort of thing the controllers control, what it means that they all seem to identify themselves by their job. The men on the site confess that they want to fall in love again, or that they're looking for a companion, or they'll baldly say *you* are the one they're looking for: My day starts off great if … I wake up beside you; sometimes it's, *waked* up next to you. Oh yeah? Sev thinks. She thinks about Ernst, Hendrik's father, about his depression. She remembers her last year with him, when she thought she'd have to sleep next to him for the rest of her life. She thinks about the other relationships she's had. She thinks about the love of her life, whom she possibly only calls the love of her life because it ended before it could fizzle out; it never had the chance to definitively fail. She has no idea how it's supposed to work, this being together, sharing a life.

"My fist hungers for justice!" Hendrik calls in a muffled voice, as if his cry is coming from far away, through the fog of battle. On stocking feet she weaves her way through his toys. In the kitchen she makes herself a cup of coffee, and a cup of cocoa for him.

She's lived with three men. The first was Felix, she was twenty-five and had only recently broken up with Jasja, the boy she shamelessly called the love of her life, even to Felix's face. The relationship with Jasja had been an open one, they didn't live together, there were other hookups, but then they would tell each other about them, which only made the intimacy between the two of them deeper than with anyone else. Jasja was intense, energetic, original, emotional. He was intelligent, but his intelligence was scattered. He changed his mind about what he wanted to study from year to year: philosophy, Dutch, Russian, history, the violin at the conservatory. They were together, or more or less together, from age eighteen to twenty-three. She was crazy about him, she felt understood and deeply connected, but also uneasy about that fickleness of his. Her girlfriends thought he took advantage of her; she didn't have the words to contradict them. The fact that she was sometimes unhappy when Jasja was with someone else proved, they said, that when she said sexual fidelity wasn't important to her, she was just fooling herself. She was very young, he too, she wishes she could do it all over again, but there isn't a box to check off for that sort of thing on dating sites.

She sees the milk for the cocoa bubbling up in the pan and foaming over the brim. By the time she springs into action, the spill has quenched the gas flame, and the smell of scalded milk rises from the hob. Some of the things in her apartment were well maintained only during the four years she lived with Ernst. He used to polish the cooker hood with a special product, he scratched the candlewax off the candlesticks, watered the plants, sometimes he even starched the bed linens. She dabs at the brown gunk with a paper towel and burns her hand on the metal. She holds her hand under running water until all sensation is gone.

After Jasja left, she tried a more traditional model with Felix. She and Felix did things together. They bought a house, renovated that house. They learned to ski and play bridge, they invited friends for dinner, they were tennis partners. She accepted the fact that there was a whole river coursing between their living-together arrangement and her private thoughts and feelings, a river that was rarely bridged; she assumed it was the same for him. She was a grown-up, she felt grown up, she thought it would be easy for her to fill in the traditionally established contours of adulthood. They talked about having children. They decided to wait until they were in their thirties. She didn't really want to have children, but as long as her thirties were some way off, she thought it was fine to keep that thought on her side of the river. After five years, just before her thirtieth birthday, Felix left her. He had found someone else. He told Sev that she didn't need him at all. It was an accusation, and also an explanation. She was sad. She felt uprooted, anyway. Was it true she didn't need anybody? Really? In what way should she have needed him? How did other people need other people? Was it something to aspire to? They sold the house; she rented a studio in the city center that never became a cozy or comfortable home. She worked, she earned money, had boyfriends, never for very long, sometimes two at a time. She spent a week with Jasja when he was in the Netherlands before moving to Canada for good, and at the end of that week, the emptiness felt infinitely worse than it had after Felix's departure. She bought her current apartment.

She leaves the mug and a saucer with biscuits on the floor next to her son, fondles a head that is immediately twisted away, out of reach—no cuddling during military campaigns!—and sits down at the window again.

At the end of a talk she gave, she met Johan. He offered to buy her a drink and explained to her what was so great about her. As she was putting on her coat, he asked if he could come.

"Come?" she asked. "Where?"

"With you."

"I'm going home."

"Then take me home, home with you." It slammed through her body like a wave.

"Come then, come with me," she said, looking at him, "come home with me then." And that's how it started. He was thirteen years younger than her and had just started university. He looked up to her, not the way she would look up to someone if she were in his place; it would have paralyzed her on the outside and made her balk on the inside, and she'd have beaten an immediate retreat, but Johan loved seeing her as his better, he basked in her radiance, he asked her questions, admired her eagerly and extravagantly, and in bed he was wonderfully diligent. She paid the bills, took him along to dinners and performances. He looked up to her, but she did not look down on him, she admired his grace, his devotion, he was funny and smart. For the first time since Jasja, she didn't feel the need to follow the generally accepted confines within which relationships were supposed to take place. And she also realized that refusing to do so didn't mean a lack of commitment, as in the on-and-off relationships she'd had since Felix. Once she came home when Johan was having some fellow students over. She was shocked by how very young they were, how much younger than she was, something she no longer noticed about Johan himself.

She happened to bump into him on the street a few weeks ago; they hadn't seen each other in at least five years. He lives with someone called Frederieke, they have a baby. Sev took him home with her, the way she'd taken him home back in the day: a tribute, a small homage to the memory, and they slept together, also in homage to the memory. How does that work, time, she wondered; he had lived here in this apartment with her once, now he was back again, the exact age she'd been then, they had both had a baby. He was exhausted from the sleepless nights, he told her. Nights spent in bed beside Frederieke, she thought to herself. She touched his curls, she stroked his soft young skin, he felt familiar to her fingers, and it was as if something opened up somewhere inside her, as if her body were waking up from a slumber she hadn't realized she was in. Ah yes, that's who you are, they kept telling each other, ah yes, that's what you like, as she licked his neck like an animal. This, she thought to herself, this once a week, not a relationship, let him just stay with his Frederieke and their child, but once a week let him come and make love to me like this. The thought made her cry, but she hid her tears because she didn't expect he'd want to start an affair with her if he thought she was emotionally unstable or lonely, and because she wouldn't know how to convince him they were tears of joy. Afterward they took a shower together, she made a pot of tea, they showed each other pictures of their children on their phones, they stared out the window and then said goodbye.

As it turned out, he wasn't interested in having an affair with her at all; as far as he was concerned it was just that one time, he texted her back. She signed up for the dating site that very day. What she wanted wasn't a companion, or someone to wake up next to. Did she want to fall in love again? She didn't know, what she wanted was skin, a warm body, someone else's desire, her own desire. Not a relationship, relationships were too complicated, and sooner or later turned into a tangle of responsibilities and obligations. A lover was what she wanted, but a kind one, and preferably with a cultured mind.

After the year with Johan, she'd been alone for a spell; she would see Jasja every so often when he was in the Netherlands, and then he would stay at her place. She met Ernst at a party. He wasn't ambitious, he was a dreamer, gentle, caring. They were both thirty-five. Perhaps she wanted to have a baby after all. This was her chance.

"Mom?"

"Hendrik."

"Can I go see if Simon's home?"

"Yes, you may."

"And if he isn't home, can I go see if Koen's home?"

"Yes, and if he isn't in either, you're coming straight back home again, okay?"

He puts on his sneakers and goes out.

The photos from the time Ernst lived here depict a sense of calm and happiness that she can't remember. The house looks cozier, with pictures on the wall and their belongings displayed in such a way that clutter isn't clutter but a carefully curated still life. The whole thing radiates serenity and tenderness, it all speaks of warmth, caring and love. Snapshots of Hendrik on Ernst's lap, or Hendrik on Sev's lap, nursing, asleep, in the bath, in bed, on a blanket in a park. And it must have been the truth—in the moments recorded for posterity, anyway. When Ernst was too ill to get out of bed for days at a time, and she had put Hendrik on his chest and taken a picture, maybe in order to show it to him, maybe to push him to get up and *do* something, what you see in that little relic of just one moment is a baby's soft little body lying on the father's large warm body.

The manager has sent her a message. She's asked what he's a manager of, and his reply is: people, and what those people do or make doesn't matter. "Computers, cancer patients, automobiles, as far as I'm concerned, it's all the same." He asks if she owns a lot of shoes, and how long she's been divorced. She says she doesn't have very many shoes and asks if his divorce has shaken his belief in romantic love. She doesn't want anyone who believes in romantic love.

Not staying means leaving

His friend spoke to her. Or, rather, he was speaking to Tirza, but he was looking at her at the same time. And *he* also looked at her, Rafik; now she knows his name. His friend asked what they were doing, where they lived, which school they went to, if they were sisters. Tirza stuck her nose in the air. *Moroccers*, she scoffed as they walked back, as if that explained it. Anyway, Krista had tried to compensate for Tirza's snootiness by trying to look friendly; maybe he was too. The fact the two of them hadn't really joined in the conversation meant they were having a kind of conversation of their own, a silent conversation, a conversation without words. She doesn't think she looked as good as she wished she'd looked. She can't wait to get upstairs, to look at herself in the mirror and see what he saw, to gauge how bad it was. She can make her face do exactly what it was doing when she said hello, she needs to see what that looked like. Rafik, a name like a color, like a bird, Krista and Rafik. His eyes brown, but green too, the way his neck rises out of his shirt in the hollow of his coat, his skinny chest, Rafik, the name of a prince, a hero, a knight in shining armor. Fire.

In the front hall she hears them fighting. She can't make out what they're saying but she does hear her own name. Dad is doing most of the talking. They'll shut up as soon as she walks in the room, they think they can hide it from her, they've been fighting for days, and her dad has slept on the couch two nights already. Her mother's beige coat hanging from the coatrack drags up something hazy, a flashback from the past, how long has she had that coat? It reminds Krista of swimming lessons, of sitting in the front seat when she wasn't really supposed to, her mother whispering something in her ear, a winter vacation in Rome, the Colosseum, crisp winter air, her mother with her dad's arm around her holding Krista's hand, Ally's head on her lap, reading to them about the wild animals and the gladiators who met their end down there in the arena.

When she opens the door her father looks up. He's standing by the table, balled fist about to slam down on it. Her mother sitting across from him, her head in her hands. His arm freezes in midair. Terri, startled at the sudden silence, looks slowly up at him, then at her.

"Hi, Kris."

"Don't mind me, pound the table if you want."

Her father stares at his fist.

"Yes. We're having a row." Duh.

"I'll be upstairs."

"Kris."

"Yeah?" They'd better not start giving her grief about her coat, telling her to hang it up, she needs to see herself in her coat, with her coat on, with her coat on exactly the way Rafik saw her.

"It happens."

"Really."

"Don't worry. We'll make up again."

"Whatev."

"What?"

"Makes no difference to me."

"Sorry?"

"Go ahead, I don't *care!*"

"Kris!" Her mother's not going to leave it there. She's already halfway up the stairs. "Come back here."

"Why."

"Your tone of voice. Your attitude. Your coat."

She zips her mouth, stares at her mother. Her angry mother. She hasn't the foggiest why she's so angry at her dad. Terri wants them all to behave the way she does, or the way she expects them to. She wants Krista to study Russian or Italian later, just because she wishes she'd done it herself, and because she claims Kris has her knack for languages. That's such a bogus idea, that you're supposed to inherit your parents' talents and traits, it's just a way to keep children prisoner. They don't know a thing about her.

If she apologizes, she'll be able to escape.

"Sorry, Mom."

"All right, Kris."

Incredible, the way parents accept two-faced BS as good manners.

"Aren't you going to hang up your coat?"

"No, Mommy. I still need it. I'll hang it up later."

"All right, Kris."

What asinine crap. She pastes on her sweetest smile.

"Could you keep the shouting down a bit? I'd like to get my homework done." Before Terri can respond, she turns and stalks on, slams her bedroom door shut as hard as she can, and locks it. Slowly she wheels around to face the closet door. Krista, as seen by Rafik. Rafik, entranced by her gaze. Music, violins or something, or maybe Arabic chants, street litter eddying across the ground in the wind, the sun breaking through the clouds at that very moment, setting their hair aflame. No Tirza, no Mohammed, the square transformed into a wide-open plain, the houses into mountains. Fingernails scratching at her door.

"What do you want?"

"Mommy and Daddy are fighting."

"Yeah, so what, let them."

"What do you think's going on?"

"No idea."

"I think Mommy has a lover."

"Gross. Really?"

"Yeah. Daddy's yelling about her lover."

"Probably."

"Also about that guy or that philosopher or that bastard."

"Let it go, Ally."

"Can I come sit in your room?"

"No."

"Do you think they'll get divorced?"

"No."

"Why not?"

"They don't dare."

"Won't you be upset if they get divorced?"

"Losers." She shrugs her shoulders.

"You don't have to mind me. I'll just sit on your bed and I promise to be quiet."

"I said no." Kris shuts the door. Ally stands in the corridor, not knowing what to do. She can't explain why divorce is one of the worst things she can think of. Now there's music coming from Krista's room. Ally slinks back to her own domain. A lover. She looks it up; of all the definitions, *extramarital romantic partner* seems the most applicable. The word is too pretty for what it means. She thinks about Marina Flakovitz, about the way she looks when she's hitting the ball, everything about her is power and aim and concentration. She returns to the landing, lies down with her head cantilevered over the stairs, her hair sweeping the treads, she can feel the prickly sisal through her clothes. Her dad is saying her mom should tell *the children*. And her mom says she doesn't know *what* she should tell them, she says no *decision*'s been made yet. And then she says she doesn't know if she can stay. Ally and her dad both hold their breath, get low on oxygen, start to grow dizzy. What does that mean, can't stay? Not staying means leaving. Her dad says she should hurry up and think of *something*, come to some decision. Her mom says she always has to take care of everything by herself and then her father starts laughing but

it isn't a happy laugh and Ally cringes with—
what is it?—shame. She slinks back to her
bedroom.

WINTER

We have something to tell you

David takes the egg-white meringues out of
the oven and turns up the heat. He sautés the
onion and garlic, adds the pepper and thyme,
then slices the celery, carrot, and bell pepper.
Terri is going around picking up papers and
other junk left lying around, depositing the
little piles on the stairs, one stair tread per
family member. He adds the diced vegetables to the onions. She tosses something in
the garbage and smoothly shuts a cupboard
door he's left open with a shrug of her hip. He
starts to fry the bacon in the other pan, and

then cooks the sausages in the rendered grease; she gathers discarded shoes and lines them up in the front hall, beneath the coatrack; he slides the duck legs into the remaining fat.

"I think Simone doesn't eat pork anymore." She points at the bacon and the sausage in passing.

"Oh. Why not? So suddenly? Are you sure?"

"Almost sure."

"Is it a diet? Or a religious thing?" He pours some broth into the pan, adds tomatoes, tomato puree and a bay leaf, drains the liquid the beans have been soaking in, adds those to the pan, and tosses everything together. "Did she convert to Judaism?"

"Do you want me to ask her?"

"Or Islam? No, don't ask." Cassoulet without pork. Simone and Hugo are their best friends. David's known Hugo since their finals year, nearly thirty years ago. They got married the same year, their children are about the same age. He can't remember Simone ever not eating pork. How does Terri know?

"Has she ever mentioned it to you? Not in connection with this dinner, I mean? Or any other meal? Apart from any meal, I mean? How did you find out?"

"Sorry?"

"How did you find out?" She has a stack of newspapers in her arms, unread newspapers, he has no time for the world. Hunger, business, war, it all pales in comparison to *his* problems.

"How did I find out what?"

"It must be a new fad. No pork."

"Do you want to keep any of these?"

"Haven't read any of them."

"Right. Do you want to save any?"

He shakes his head. Now that his marriage is no longer an indisputable fact, he wonders what he really used to think of it, of this, of her. Was it really always the life he'd wanted, wasn't every concession made in exchange for the promise of lifelong commitment? And what does he know about his best friend's marriage? A good marriage, he'd have said only a month ago, but he's no longer sure of anything now. What makes a marriage a good one, what makes it so you never bring up the subject of your marriage with your best friend—not really, Hugo and he never have, anyway, perhaps because he always thought the privacy of that marriage was the overriding factor.

"Did you just ask me how I know?" He nods. She shakes her head. He dumps the contents of the pan into a serving dish and starts grinding a few rusks into crumbs, using a small bowl inside a bigger one as a mortar.

"Do we have a plan? Do we just tell them as soon as we're all sitting down? Are you going to tell them? I think you should tell them."

"Yes, I think so too. I'll tell them. You could say something too, of course."

"My side of the story."

"If you like."

He wants to say that his side of the story doesn't exist, that's the problem. Perhaps she'll say she hasn't been happy for a while. Should he then say that he wasn't very happy either, but that until the moment she dropped her bombshell, it hadn't seemed a relevant issue? Happy, unhappy, what does it mean? They were simply living their life. And there was love. What else could it have been? Has Simone ever had an affair, has Hugo ever cheated on her?

"I'm not going to tell them very much."

"No."

"They'll have something to say, I presume."

"They'll have questions."

"Perhaps."

"They're our friends, after all."

She doesn't say anything. She stands there cradling the newspapers in her arms. He stops whisking the sauce.

"Are you done with our friends now too?"

"I don't know, David, it's just that those friends belong to the way it used to be, to what I don't want anymore."

It's getting dark outside.

"Terri?" He starts twisting the corkscrew into the bottle. She is stuffing the papers into a bag; the bag is too small, it's not going to work, it's already ripping on one side. "Is this the first time you've cheated on me?"

"Oh, shit, this isn't working!"

He takes a larger, sturdier bag from the cupboard and tosses it in her direction, but as a symbol of his complete lack of strength and clout, the thing flutters to the floor between them like a deflated kite. It's a French supermarket bag; every year they lug bottles of crémant and wine and sausage and cheese and cornichons and tea and soap home with them from France in those shopping bags. Summer vacations. What happens to those now?

"Is this the first time you've been unfaithful to me, Terri? Were you happy with me, with us, all this time, and then you just suddenly fell in love with someone else, and that changed everything for you—is that it?"

"No, that's not it."

"Are you leaving me for Lucas?"

"No."

"Aren't you? In effect."

"No."

"How come no?"

"It isn't that I'm going to do the, what's it called, the thing or whatever it's supposed to be, with him, now."

"The thing or whatever it's supposed to be."

"Right." She's wedging the newspapers into the grocery bag.

"But you are, aren't you?"

"No. I never want to do this again, the way we were."

"But you did want it at first, didn't you, and for a long time? The way it was? You're just as responsible for making this life the way it is now as I am." He starts following her about the room. "You're the one who changed. How did that happen, how come you suddenly changed like that? How could I ever have anticipated that?"

"I'll just go take this out, the glass too." She stuffs her phone in her pocket, as if you need a phone when heading out to the recycling bins, and leaves him standing in the kitchen, in the middle of the kitchen that, when they bought the house ten years ago, opting for the convenience of a new housing development over inner city charm, was described as *the heart of the home*. There he stands, with a wooden spoon in his hand, stuck in the middle of the heart of the home.

The oysters have been slurped, and they're updating each other on the children. Hugo and Simone have discovered that their eldest daughter Jane skips school and smokes weed at recess. She was given a two-day suspension, but since they both had to go to work, it only freed her up to do whatever she wanted. They're worried.

"Then I'll see her lolling on the sofa staring at her phone with those glassy eyes and that secretive grin, and she's there, right there in front of me, but her whole life is happening out of my sight."

"Is she stoned when she's home, then?"

"Yes, every time I see that sweet smile on her face I now think she's stoned, that's right, because normally she's just a sulky teenager."

David is relieved that their kids don't do that, they're more levelheaded, or, how to put it, he's aware of all the terrible things that can happen these days; all those years of stable family happiness have given them a good foundation. They're past the age of twelve; he's read that you only have influence over your children before their twelfth birthday, so before they've passed that milestone you'd better have crammed all the important stuff into them, from brushing their teeth twice a day to building their self-esteem.

"But we used to smoke when we were seventeen too, didn't we?" says Hugo.

Well, maybe *you* did, thinks David.

"Yeah, but it was a different time."

"And the weed was more innocuous, it didn't make you psychotic."

"Is she already seventeen, then?"

"Is it making her psychotic?"

"No. No, she's sixteen and no no no, she isn't psychotic, but you read it can lead to that. I've read it. It's terrifying."

"Why does she do it?" asks Terri.

"Why?"

"Yeah, is it rebellion, peer pressure? Or is she unhappy?"

"No, God, I don't know. Hard to say ... I'd say it's her friends, but maybe that's too easy. Simone?"

"I don't know either. I just don't know. You don't know what they're thinking anymore, at that age. Don't you have the same problem?"

"Krista and Ally are very open with us."

"Well ..." Is Terri going to contradict him now, publicly? Is that part of the new deal too? "You don't know what they *aren't* telling us."

"No, you don't know. You never know." The same goes for people who aren't your children, David thinks, your friends, your significant other, or the one who's supposed to be your significant other, you have no idea what's being stifled and concealed, what may be brewing or rotting. He gets up to take the cassoulet out of the oven, fetches the red wine, puts out clean glasses, and refills the water carafe. Terri stays seated.

"Jane has always been a little freedom fighter, she always mastered anything increasing her autonomy very early: walking, going potty. Milo's another story … But you want her to find safe ways to navigate it—drugs, I don't know, it's about casting off the restraints, of course, she'll be having sex next, who knows, I don't know, we just don't know."

"No, no, definitely not, not that, not yet anyway. Kids are awfully prudish these days."

"How do you know?"

"Statistics."

"That's never a good argument, Hugo. Help me, Terri."

"Right. No, Hugo, you really can't bring in statistics. They're useless when it comes to the individual case."

"Probability. Weighing the chances. Of course it isn't useless."

"No, really, it doesn't help, the chance she isn't average is ..."

"Small! The most likely chance is that she's just average."

"In most things she *isn't* average. We tend to count on things being above average, on the positive exception to the rule. Isn't that right, Hugo? Including us."

"As far as relationships go, moral questions, the meaning of life, she's simply a very average sixteen-year-old, conventional and straightforward."

Simone is no longer listening, she's shuddering at the implications of her own thoughts.

"She's far too young, I think."

"You know what you were like when you were sixteen."

"Yes! Completely naive! I swear!"

"Hormones. I remember those!" Hugo looks triumphant.

"We bought some condoms, we left them in a drawer."

"One pack?" Terri asks.

"Yes."

"Containing three condoms? She'll never take them, of course, you should have bought at least a hundred and left them lying around in a box, so that if she takes one out it won't be noticed."

Oh God, thinks David, turning to the sink, a big box of condoms, Terri's got condoms on her mind, does she practice safe sex with that asshole? As if he cares, she no longer sleeps with him anyway. It makes him sick to think of her private parts, and someone else taking his pleasure there, as if it besmirched *him*, as if the guy were touching *him*. And he thinks about Jane, and about Krista and their developing bodies. Oh God, oh God, he thinks, they're entering this phase now, the girls, another thing he'll have to deal with on his own because their mother has cast off all restraint herself, is that hormonal too?

"David!"

"Sorry? What?"

"The faucet!" He's left the faucet running, standing right next to it, wearing two oven mitts and with no idea what he was doing before glazing over. Terri shuts the faucet and turns off the oven. She carries the salad to the table, then the bread and the water carafe, and puts down two tile trivets. She touches his back.

"Come," she says softly, "come, come on." Something between an invitation and a warning. It makes him go weak in the knees.

He sets down the hot casserole on the tiles.

"There, nobody's become vegetarian all of a sudden, I hope? I just heard you don't eat pork any more, Simone, but I'd already started cooking."

"Yes, but I'm not strict about it."

"You can just fish out the sausage."

The two families have gone on vacation together several times. Terri and David used to feel rather smug, thinking they were happier, or better, than Simone and Hugo. Going on vacation with other people is a way of keeping your worst habits in check; with other people's eyes on you, you feel less free to behave as you like, a function spouses cease fulfilling for each other after a few years of marriage. And it's a way to gussy up the picture of your own life a bit. I'm glad you're not as much of a dolt as Hugo, Terri would say, for example. I'm glad you make me laugh, David would tell her then, sniffing the mountain breeze in her hair, pressing his face into her warm sunbaked neck, expressing his delight that the children no longer slept in their room, and starting to take her clothes off.

"I've been to a naturopath, who gave me a list of things I ought to avoid. Pork is one of them. Alcohol too, actually."

"Oh dear."

"I went to him because I was so tired all the time."

"Oh. Poor you."

"Oh well, I'm not *that* tired." She raises her glass. They laugh. They toast. To their friendship. They all help themselves, Hugo says it smells wonderful, it's delicious. David looks at Terri, who has helped herself to a minuscule dollop. Is this the moment? She nods curtly at him, a touch of irritation on her face.

"Sleep."

"Excuse me?"

"Sleep, you need to get more sleep, nobody gets enough sleep. Nobody in the Western world gets enough sleep."

"Never start a sentence with 'nobody in the Western world,' Hugo."

"Ah, no—uh—but it definitely *is* a problem."

The conversation meanders through the topics they always seem to cover, acquaintances and friends in common, the parents, what they've read, what they ought to read, stuff they've recently bought, a sofa for Hugo and Simone, and the shirt Terri is wearing tonight that David hadn't noticed as being new.

"That's such a lovely fabric." Yeah, yeah, lovely fabric. David gazes at them, no longer joining in the conversation; he feels something hysterical brewing at the back of his throat. He remembers the first time Hugo told him about Simone, about her heavy dark hair, and about them kissing. How very little he and Hugo used to tell each other back in those days, or in the years since. He knows nothing. They help themselves to seconds, and the glasses are refilled.

"Anyone for more salad? No? Then I'll finish it." They eat, they drink. Hugo keeps touching Simone's arm, it's a habit of his, and he doesn't seem conscious of it. They've remarked on it in the past, Terri and he. She thought it was a bit possessive. He said he would love it if someone, Terri for instance, kept putting her hand on his, in the presence of others, as a marker: you are mine. Now she'll never touch him again like that. Never touch him again. They chew, they swallow.

"We have something to tell you." Terri has finally found the lull in which to make her announcement. Hugo and Simone look from her to him and back again. Expectantly. They don't notice what he notices, that her mouth is set. Hugo even looks excited, he's anticipating some great piece of news, a move, a baby, a first novel. The thought of it makes David laugh, or something like it anyway, it may have been a hiccup. Three faces turn toward him, Terri's looks annoyed. She lets out a long breath.

"We're splitting up."

"What?" Just that one silly word, and Hugo's open mouth, from which it came. Then, silence. The candlelight, her grandmother's dishes, the greasy fingerprints on the glasses, Hugo's hand moving across the table over toward Simone's arm. The kitchen, the familiarity of it all, the strangeness of it all.

"Yes, I thought you'd be surprised." Terri pushes her plate away and crosses her arms. David clenches his hands between his legs under the table.

"May I ask ..." Hugo pulls the corners of his mouth down in an expression hovering between fear and revulsion. There's a pause until Terri finishes his sentence for him.

"Why?"

"Yes. May I ask why?"

"It's ... finished, I think that's what it's called, it's done. I'm ... done ... with it."

"Finished."

"The question why is difficult to answer, Hugo. There is no simple why."

"So there isn't ..." As a variation on Hugo's mouth contortions, now Simone's eyebrows are raised right up to her bangs. "One of you isn't ... There isn't ... There's no ..."

"One else?"

"Yes."

Terri gives a sigh. Simone's eyebrows sink into a frown, and the corners of Hugo's mouth stretch tentatively into an encouraging ghost of a smile. What's with the facial gymnastics?

"There is, yes. There is someone else, that too. But I think it's best not to go into it too much. Seeing that we've never had any *real* conversations about how things stand, which may explain why this comes as such a surprise now, it would be silly to suddenly, at the eleventh hour, begin to ..."

"Oh."

"I'm sorry." Terri gets up and starts clearing the dishes. After she's stacked all the plates on the counter, and after she's covered the leftovers in the casserole with foil and slid it back in the oven, when she's set the salad bowl with all the cutlery in the sink, she announces in a strange voice: "If you'll excuse me, I'm just going upstairs a minute." No one speaks. Terri disappears, Hugo pats his wife's hand, Simone stares at her plate, David gazes at his friends.

"Jeez, David," Hugo says.

A thing in his hands

Lucas runs his fingers down her back, across her butt. She pushes it up against his hands. It's the late afternoon, the light is the light of spring, fresh, clear, and thin. She has to go home shortly. He looks at her, he's trying to look cool, detached, but that's getting harder to do.

"I've got to go home."

"Just a few more minutes."

"I'm on child duty."

"Do you like this?"

"Yes."

They've divided up the days between them, she is there five days, and then David is on for the next nine. On the days it's David's turn, Terri's friend Sanne is letting her stay on the ground floor of her house. Sanne who looks at her with an expression that's hard to gauge. It may be disapproval, or maybe she's afraid cheating is contagious. On Terri's days, David stays in the attic of a colleague, in a poky room where, he says woefully, he sits around fretting that their whole life together may have been just a dream. Terri barely manages to get through her days with the kids, she starts hyperventilating the moment she sets foot across the threshold. The meals she cooks are complete flops, she never seems to get to the motherly things she's supposed to do, her kids annoy the hell out of her, as if they've stopped belonging to her. They use her toothbrush, they don't flush the toilet, they never pick up their belongings. Ally doesn't speak, and Krista is rude. Terri constantly feels a scream in her throat, her hand itches to smack one of them. When she's home she's on edge, overtaxed, on the verge of collapsing, exploding, imploding, disappearing. But on the days she's not at home she feels airy, she never knew there was so much space in a day, or that there was so much space inside her.

Lucas drips oil onto her back. His hands glide over her skin in circular motions, he kneads her buttocks, lets his hand slide in between. Sometimes he asks her about David, about sex with David. She doesn't like to answer. It feels like she's betraying David, or herself. David was the first man she slept with, and Lucas is the third. David doesn't know either of those facts. She was ashamed of her lack of experience, so she never told him he'd been the first; her affair of five years ago was short-lived and remained superficial, it would have been needlessly provocative to tell him about it. Sex with David was consistent, without any great lulls; it was relatively uncomplicated. They had perfected the techniques for satisfying each other, it was efficient, it relaxed her, the way they did it gave her leeway to think of other men. He usually took a shower beforehand and she did the same afterwards. It didn't touch her soul. Not just later on, but never. She thinks this is probably the first time she's been a true adult. Or, indeed, been truly awake.

"And this?"

"Yes."

"Do you like this too?"

"This too." And now she's forty-five, she keeps thinking, now she is forty-fucking-five. A throttling rage wells up in her throat. When she was young there were always boys in love with her, she was a popular girl, she'd never done much with it, considering it more a boost to her standing than something she actually took pleasure in. She was kissed, certainly, there was a great deal of kissing, with all sorts of boys, in all sorts of places, she let them do things to her, she never did much reciprocating, never went home with anyone, David was the first boyfriend who ever saw her climax. She thinks of a girl-friend who was forty before ever having an orgasm; she'd never dared to go all the way because the sensation felt too much like the run-up to a temper tantrum. This friend's tantrums were legendary and usually de-structive. Terri has had orgasms for as long as she can remember, but only now, for the first time in her life, does she feel such sickening fury, as if she's only just discovered that she's been lied to all these years. She feels, yes that's it, just as betrayed by David as he is being betrayed by her.

Lucas has positioned himself between her legs and is starting to pull her thighs wider apart. She presses her face into the pillow. He makes her wait for it. Waiting, she falls into a swoon of emptiness. When, with a single move, he breaks her trance, she starts moaning, not to encourage him, the sounds just escape from her, irrepressibly; for a split second she's mortified, and then she surrenders. The thoughts are banished from her mind, she's not a mind, she is her skin, her nerves, her thighs, her vagina, Lucas is thrusting the rage out of her body, she wants to scream, everything inside her that was stuck just lets go, she wants to be a body and nothing else, an animal, an instrument for him to play, a thing, a thing in his hands.

She gets dressed as he lies back, gazing at her.

"That was nice."

"It was."

"It was?"

"Yes."

"Why was it so nice?"

She buttons her blouse. She thinks of Krista and the way she looks at her with loathing. She thinks of David and Ally.

"Well? What was so nice about it, me jumping your bones?"

That jumping her bones promptly makes her weak-kneed.

"I've got to get home."

"You should get out of there."

"I know."

"It's no longer your home."

"I know."

"Rent a place."

"It takes time, Lucas. I want to find something with space for the girls as well. Three bedrooms. No idea what I can afford."

"Start off basing it on your own salary."

"I have a mortgage on the house."

"Then sell the house."

"Don't be so simplistic, Lucas, please, are you really that thick?"

"No darling, I'm probably not that thick,

but I wouldn't want to be as smart as you."

She kisses him, lying there flat on his back with his hands under his head, still gazing at her; he doesn't kiss her back. He takes pride in being naive about the things most people consider part of adult life.

"David doesn't want to sell the house."

"Then he should take over your portion of the mortgage."

"I don't know that he can afford it."

"If he can't, you should sell. And how do you know he can't? Figure it out. Let him figure it out."

She sighs. He sighs too.

"Lucas."

"Whatever."

"Lucas!"

"Yes, Terri."

"It just takes time. Everything."

"Yeah, I suppose." He turns and pulls the blanket up over himself. "Okay, bye. See you next time."

She makes her way down the stairs, picks up her bag of laundry and briefcase, and lets herself out. She's sobbing as she unlocks her bike. She rides to the end of the street, pedals the incline up to the bridge as if it's a descent into the underworld where it's dark and the air is thin. She has tried explaining it to David: how to her, it's better to keep moving than to stand still. He gets furious when she says their life has grown stagnant, he doesn't think it's stagnant, he says what she calls stagnation is just tranquility and that tranquility is a kind of happiness, or a different phase of happiness—how did he put it again? It's the form their life has taken, anyway, and she can't unilaterally end the reality they've created together. He claims he has a veto.

Ahead of her a boy and a girl ride hand in hand, blocking her way. She pictures their handlebars getting tangled, the girl's coat getting caught in the boy's spokes, the wheels swerving, the sound of metal on metal, their bones fracturing and their blushing cheeks getting skinned on the asphalt. She rubs away her tears with her sleeve. Maybe they could switch the five days to two days, and the nine days to twelve; two days she could probably manage.

"We should just tell them we don't want it, that we don't want her to come."

"But I do want her to come."

"I thought you hated having her here too."

"I want her not to be the way she is, not the way she's acting now, that's all."

"So maybe we can say that if she insists on acting the way she's been acting lately, we'd rather be alone."

"All alone?"

"You and me, that's not really alone. How bad can it be? Terri is nuts."

"Dad would come home if she left."

"Yes. Maybe we should tell David we don't want to be left alone with her."

"But then we'll be with Dad all the time."

"He's okay. Better than her."

"But don't you feel sorry for Terri?"

"Sorry? She doesn't even want to be here!"

"But we *are* her kids. She made us herself."

"She says she can't stand *this life*. Ally, what do you think that means?" Ally starts to cry. "Come on, Al, she thinks we're ruining her life."

"Us?"

"All three of us. She says so herself."

Krista fishes around in a drawer for some paper towels, a napkin, something for Ally to wipe her blubbering baby face with, she finds a bag of chips and tosses it on the table, she can't stand it when Ally acts like this, so young and helpless, and Krista feels the tentacles trapping her inside this house and this situation. She throws a tea towel at her little sister.

"Come on, monkey, time to grow up."

"Kris."

"Dry your tears. We've got to come up with a plan. She'll be here any second."

Ally used to think that all the others were only playing a role, that they were all pulling her leg, that Mrs. Brakema was really a witch disguised as the nice lady next door, that sort of thing. This unmasking of her mother, now exposed as a non-mother, as an actor fed up with her role, comes suspiciously close to her childhood fears. Krista gets terribly impatient when Ally tries telling her things like that, and she has to make sure Krista stays here, here with her, so they'll be together when Terri gets home. Right at that moment, the sound of the front door.

"I'm home!"

Krista and Ally look at each other. Ally wipes her nose on the tea towel.

"Hey, what's this, are you blowing your nose in a tea towel?"

Krista lets her head drop on the table with a bang.

"Kris!"

"Sorry, Mommy." Ally wads the tea towel into a ball. "There wasn't anything else for me to use."

"Krista!" Krista lifts her head. "Can't you be polite and say hello?"

"Be polite and say hello yourself."

Terri sits down at the table. "Okay. Let's start again, shall we?"

Nobody says anything. That used to work when she was five, Krista thinks, what does she expect? Ally starts to cry again. Terri picks up the chips, folds the bag shut, seals it with a clothespin and stows it in a cupboard.

"We were eating that."

"And now you're not."

"Is that so?"

"We're having dinner in an hour."

"What are we having?"

"No idea." She looks at the chalkboard, but it's blank. "Something healthy."

"Nice. I'll have some seaweed."

Terri hands Ally a pack of tissues, rests her hand on her daughter's soft brown hair. It seems to help; she stops crying. Terri thinks about lice, about school, about having to tell the counselors at that school that they're getting a divorce, is that what parents are supposed to do, or do you leave it to your children to tell them? Do they already know?

"Ally," says Krista, "are you coming?"

"Where are you going?"

"We were having a conversation."

"So?"

"So, we're going upstairs to finish it." Without taking her eyes off Terri, Krista gets up, snatches the bag of chips from the cupboard again, and slaps the clothespin into her mother's hand as Ally gets to her feet. Terri doesn't react, watches them go. She asks herself whom she's doing a favor by being here, acting at being the mother here, when it isn't even appreciated. David doesn't really want to have to be in that attic room, and she doesn't want to be here. Can't they just accept the situation for what it is? Can't she just go? Go back to Lucas's spotless apartment, where there's not a speck of dust, where she can be her true self? She has to take a shower, she's all sweaty. She has to shop for food, cook, eat, there's at least four hours to go before she can go to bed. She knows she loves her daughters, but she can't seem to find that sentiment inside her right now. She puts her head down on the table. Is that possible? Can you just wake up one day and find that the love is gone? Is she going insane? Is love just a habit, is that all it is? Or an effort of will? Is anything *real* at all?

"I'm calling Dad."

"I don't know."

"She's acting weird."

"You'll get him all worried."

"She didn't even try to console you!"

"Maybe she didn't notice I was crying."

"People sometimes go crazy. Out of the blue. Sometimes they go crazy and kill their children. It happens a lot."

"Don't be so creepy."

"I'm not being creepy, she's the one being creepy."

"She did put her hand on my head, you know."

"After getting mad about the tea towel and the chips."

"She put her hand very gently on my head."

"Ally, come on, please stop crying, you idiot. You've got snot coming out of your nose."

"I'm sorry." She can't stop. But it's nice to be in Krista's bedroom with her. "Sorry, Kris. But she did put her hand on my head."

"Okay, okay fine."

Dad please come home, Mom's acting weird. The message came in over an hour ago. He thinks about the mountain of work still awaiting him, about his lack of enthusiasm for that work, about the risks he's running if he doesn't do it well. The first page of his very first exercise book held the following dedication, written in fountain pen in flawlessly sloping script: *Doing what you want is tempting, it's true, but doing what you must is better for you. Good luck at school, David. Your father.* He shares this memory with Mira, the colleague sitting across from him.

"Jeez, David, that does explain everything. How awful." She has stopped typing and smiles at him over her glasses. They are quiet for a while, but don't resume the concentration their work requires.

"I'm getting divorced."

"Yes, I'd heard something like that."

"Who told you?"

"Elsbeth." He never told Elsbeth. "How awful for you."

"Yes. I've got to go home. There's a problem with the kids."

"Oh."

"I'm not supposed to be home, actually. I'm staying in Jaap's attic."

"Oh David, jeez, that must be tough, Jaap's attic. How beastly. Are you going to sell the house?"

"Yes, it's very lonely. Although it's a perfectly fine attic. We don't know. We don't know what to do next."

"Have you had any help?"

"Help?"

"A mediator. Family therapist. Financial adviser."

"We've always been very reasonable people. Both of us. Her too."

"But what's the matter with your kids now?" She's emerged from behind her desk and comes rolling towards him, chair and all.

"I don't know." He waves his phone.

"Go!"

"I should."

"Yes, of course you should, it's your kids."

"Yes."

Walking from the exit to his bike he calls Krista.

"Hey, Dad." She's whispering.

"I'm on my way."

He greets a colleague who's on his way in, miming he's sorry, pointing at his phone. He doesn't have to justify his presence or absence, but he feels guilty nonetheless. The soul of a serf, Terri would scoff fondly, in the old days anyway; now it's clear she only professed the fond part so that she could stand it, so that she could tolerate him, cognitive dissonance, liking what you despise because otherwise you're caught in a hopeless trap.

"What's going on?"

"Mom is mad."

"At you?"

"At us. At everybody."

"I'll be there in twenty minutes." He pedals as fast as he can, leaving the city behind, across the bridge.

Fuck you

She scoops the fries into a serving dish, divides the meat and beets among the four plates, pours water into glasses, mixes mayonnaise and yogurt in a bowl, opens the jar of fruit compote. She's done her best. She could have made the compote herself but didn't deem it necessary. She lights a candle. David comes in and looks at the food. At her. He's traded his work clothes for white shorts and a faded T-shirt. He takes a beer from the fridge and pours it into a glass. He says it looks delicious. Terri calls upstairs. Ally and

Krista sit down at their places. Krista is wearing eye makeup.

They eat. Ally quizzes her parents on the Greek gods, David is pleased with himself because he got more answers right than Terri, but tells himself he wouldn't be so pleased if she didn't so very clearly think herself intellectually superior. She may think he's stagnating, but his reservoir of knowledge is enormous. That's just the way it is. Krista pokes at her food, gazing around the table with a sullen expression, which Terri is the only one to comment on. David looks at his wife. What's changed, he wonders; the question is like an itch. What's changed, what makes this meal different from the thousands of times they've sat around this table just like this? Maybe it's the terrifying loneliness he's feeling, the realization there's something that's there only as long as you don't stop believing in it. That as soon as you stop believing in it, all you are is a collection of individual lives and secret thoughts that once cohered only by dint of some force that's now been squashed.

"Greek gods—that means you're interested in taking Latin and Greek, doesn't it?"

"I just like them."

"You used to like them when you were little too."

Krista glares at her. It's puberty, Terri thinks, it's puberty and not a total personal rejection of me, because she hates me, because she thinks I'm an idiot, she's only a child but she's forgotten that.

Tomorrow is her mother's birthday, they're all going to visit her. Terri is sleeping here tonight, David too, they're driving up to Wassenaar as a family, and for the sake of some kind of harmony, that family has to start pulling itself together now. Her parents don't know yet. Should she tell the kids to keep it under their hats? Should she call her parents tonight? Each option is as unthinkable as the next. Her mother will start to cry, and her father will think it's David's fault; there will be other guests there tomorrow, there won't be time to talk, it will ruin her mother's afternoon. It would be simplest if the children just didn't come, but she won't let Krista off the hook that easily, and since the start of the crisis Ally's been clinging to the idea of family like a banded mongoose. Thursday or Friday, or whenever it was, Terri caught her leafing through their wedding album; when they got married Ally hadn't even been born! Maybe David had taken it out, trying to get to the bottom of the debacle, trying to understand how that from-this-day-forward can go up in smoke before its time, and had left it lying around on the coffee table. They are both equally sentimental, those two. She must call her sister, Lotte, and make sure she's aware their parents don't know yet.

"The middle finger comes from ancient Greece too, did you know that?" David says.

"What do you mean, the middle finger?"

"Giving it. Giving someone the finger."

"What did it mean, then?"

"The same thing."

"Fuck you."

"Right." David stands up to get another beer from the fridge, triumphant about this silly little fact. Ally looks at him, Krista looks down at her plate, David looks at his wife, Terri looks at her eldest daughter.

"Krista, eat!"

"I hate beets."

"You used to love beets."

"You used to love Dad too."

Ally finishes the fruit compote. David slowly pours the beer into his glass and then crushes the can in his hand. Terri pokes at her food just as listlessly and unhappily and angrily as her eldest daughter. The fact that David is mad at her, sneers at her, criticizes her, is trying impress on her that she's not entitled to her own life, that her feelings have to be put to a vote before they're allowed to exist, all that is understandable, no matter how ghastly, but why must she justify herself to her fifteen-year-old daughter? What does *she* know about life, about love, about her parents, about her as a person, as an individual?

"We should talk about tomorrow."

No one speaks up.

"We've got to talk about it. I think it's best if we don't say anything. It just isn't a good idea to tell them with everybody else there. I'd rather do it by myself. At a quieter time."

"Do it by yourself?"

"Yes, or with you."

"Which would probably affect the story a bit."

"Yes."

Silence.

"They're my parents."

"Yes."

Silence.

"Okay, then are we agreed?"

"May I be excused?"

Terri doesn't respond. No one responds. After a while Krista stands up, grabs her phone from the basket and goes upstairs.

"I'm getting the key Monday." Let's just stick to practical matters, then, for God's sake.

"Oh."

"I was wondering if you could help me with some of the heavy stuff."

"I'm working Monday, as always."

"Afterwards."

"I'd like to be excused too. Okay?"

"Okay. No dessert?"

"No, thank you." Ally carries her plate to the sink and goes upstairs.

"Don't you think it's hurtful, to talk about that key, Terri? Don't you think it's insensitive?"

"The whole thing is hurtful. But not on account of the key."

"Oh, so the whole thing is hurtful to you too, is it?"

"Yes. It's extremely hurtful, for instance, that no one says anything."

"No one says anything?"

"Except for saying 'fuck you' has existed since the ancient Greeks." She looks as if she'd like to smack him. He could throttle her.

Tonight, Krista thinks, when they're all asleep, she's sneaking out to meet up with him … She puts her phone on the pillow and gets under the covers. He, Rafik, texted her, saying that he'd really like to see her, that he wants to meet her at the acoustic wall, if she likes, at midnight, or sooner, as soon as she can. He signed it with some Arabic words that she looked up on Google Translate, they mean "sweeter than honey." She reads it over again and again and again. She thinks of his dark-brown eyes, his hair, his trace of a moustache; she doesn't know how old he is, he must be seventeen or maybe even eighteen, he's so serious and so amazing, and he's interested in her, Krista, he's discovered something in her, and she'd so love to know what it is. She folds up her tongue inside her mouth and sucks up through it, moving it as if she's French-kissing him. Would she dare? Tirza did it once, it was no big deal, she said. She should have asked Tirza to tell her more about it, now she doesn't know a thing, or not enough, anyway. She picks up her phone. *I want you here on your knees with my prick in your mouth.* For a heart-stopping second she thinks it's from Rafik, but then realizes it isn't her phone, it's not hers, the blood rushes to her cheeks, it's her mother's phone! She flings the cellphone away from her and jumps out of bed, doesn't know what to do, stares at the phone on the bed as if it's a grenade missing its pin. Her mother on her knees ... She feels her own knees buckle, vomit rising into her throat. She pulls on a different pair of jeans, a clean black T-shirt. She inspects her face in the mirror, fluffs her auburn curls. Thank God, she doesn't detect any Terri-traits. She hears loud voices downstairs. They're having another fight, her father the pathetic loser and her mother the whore. She unlocks the phone by punching in her parents' wedding date. Lucas, her mother's lover, or her boyfriend, or that bastard, or the philosopher. With her face half-averted, she reads snippets of messages, stuff about her mother's body, stuff he wants to do with her. She types *Tonight I'm sucking my husband's cock* in the message box, deletes it, if only Tirza was here, she'd make her do it, for a dare. And then she deletes the entire conversation. *Are you sure you want to delete all messages in this chat?* Yep. No going back. To think she has the guts! Should she delete some of the other chats, so that it'll look as if a Pacman-like virus has chomped its way through the phone? Will her mother suspect it was her? Or will she think it was the work of some higher power? She'll probably try to blame David. She deletes Lucas's phone number from the address book. She's *got* to tell Tirza. She puts on some more mascara. She thinks she looks pretty good.

As she's going downstairs, her parents stop talking. They're still seated at the table; her dad has opened a bottle of wine, he's holding it in his right hand, his glass in his left. The beer cans are still on the table, and their plates too. Her mother is crying. Krista stares at her mouth, her wet, open mouth. It makes her want to throw up. She's got to find a way to switch the phones. Are her parents going to fight all night, is David going to sleep on the couch, will she even be able to sneak out tonight?

"Are you coming for some dessert? There's ice cream."

"Actually, uh, no. I was wondering if I really have to come, tomorrow? I'd rather go to Wassenaar another time. It'll be such a big party, who's even going to notice if I'm there or not? And I do have a lot of homework." Terri stares at her.

"Oh yeah?"

"Yeah."

"Well." It doesn't look as if she's going to answer.

"I'm just going over to Tirza's."

"What about that homework, then?"

"I've got to get a book from her. Then I'll start on it." Sidling over to the basket, she quickly switches the two phones. Fingerprints, she thinks.

"Back soon."

"What do you think she's up to?" Terri asks when the front door slams shut.

"Picking up a book at Tirza's," David says, distracted. Where were they? Terri had started crying, saying she was terribly unhappy, and that meant so much more to him than all the blame and accusations of the past weeks. In that chink in her armor, he spies a chance: if she is so unhappy, then this can't be the solution, obviously. In which case it isn't inevitable, in which case the whole thing could still be seen as just a whim.

"Where were we?"

"Nowhere. It's all pointless."

"You said you were unhappy."

"Yes."

"Won't you tell me why you're unhappy?"

"No, I just am."

"Please talk to me, try."

"No."

"Isn't that Lucas joker making you happy?"

"Don't say 'that Lucas joker.'"

"Isn't Lucas making you happy?"

"Lucas has nothing to do with it."

"How can that be? Lucas is …"

"Leave him out of it."

"But if it weren't for him …"

"Then it would have been something else."

"I don't believe that."

"Oh no?"

"No." He's inadvertently started shouting again. "It's an ordinary crush, and an ordinary midlife crisis, I wish you'd gone bloody skydiving or some other cliché, not this cliché, and don't tell me it isn't true!"

"It isn't true."

"Liar."

"I've woken up. Our life is a lie. A feeble imitation of a life. I'm unhappy."

"Terri."

"Lucas was just the catalyst."

He shrieks. "You were happy. Admit you used to be happy."

"I was, yes, but not anymore."

"Until when."

"Two years ago, I think, I don't know exactly."

"So what happened then?"

"Nothing."

"Nothing?"

"The tank just got empty, David, that's all."
He can't believe it.

"I don't want you to sleep here."

"Okay. Then I'll be going." She takes her phone and her keys, nothing else, and stalks out the door. She can't go to Sanne's, they're feuding. Sanne disapproves of what she's been doing, she's no longer a friend but a member of the jury. She takes her bike. She doesn't want to go to Lucas. She does want to go to Lucas. She doesn't want to go to Lucas just because she has nowhere else to go. She wants to *choose* him, not to latch on to him as the easy way out, she's promised herself that she'll go to him only if she really wants to be with him. Up until now she's almost always wanted to, but right now she's feeling tired and drained and ugly, and she'll have to get back here early in the morning, for the car, for the birthday gift, to change into a dress instead of jeans. On Monday she's picking up the keys to her apartment, three doors down from where she used to live when she was twenty, her life is running in a circle. What if she hadn't left, what if Lucas hadn't been in the picture, what if David were less apathetic, less afraid, what if she'd never met him, what if she'd discovered the power of sex earlier in life? What if life is just a chain of coincidences, what if this is it, what if she wants to go back now and everything's already ruined? She need only think of David's hurt face to know she doesn't ever want to go back. She dismounts and walks into the supermarket to buy cigarettes and a lighter. What if she started smoking again, after seventeen years, why not? Sitting on a wooden bench overlooking the river, she lights up, inhales, and takes out her phone to read what Lucas has written.

The bottle of wine is empty, he's a little unsteady on his feet, but he's feeling a lot better anyway. Terri hasn't come back, the girls are asleep, it's eleven o'clock. In bed with the laptop on his knees, he's wrestling his way through a ludicrous psychological test, one section of which involves choosing between two pictures. Round or square? Arrow pointing left or right? Castle or farm? Rose or tulip? Something blue or something red? Then he makes a stab at creating a profile. Man seeking woman. He tries to write something dashing and fun about himself. It isn't easy, what's so fun about him again? Under *I used to think that ...* he writes, *I would stay married to the same woman all my life.* Then he starts to cry. But it could be the wine. He flips through the profiles of the women in his category, between the ages of forty and fifty-five (or is forty too young?), within a twenty-five-kilometer radius, with or without children, and not interested in having babies. There's a lot of them, they are all looking for someone, maybe even for him, he reads variations on the tune of *My life is great, rich and fulfilled, but something's missing, maybe it's you, and maybe it's love.* The idea of having sex with someone else, free of obligations, gives him both a hard-on and a stomachache. He adds a photo, the picture Terri took of him in Berlin. He's squinting a bit in the sun, he's looking happy, unshaven and relaxed, more virile than he really is. *Are you the man who will make my life complete?* No, not that kind of man. *My soul mate?* He thought he was, once; he probably isn't yours. *Are you the woman who will help me forget all my troubles for a while?* You can't write that, that's terrible. He hears footsteps on the stairs; has Terri come home? If she has, he'll make her leave, he'll say she'd better go if she doesn't want him to hit her. He jumps out of bed and rushes out. He hears the footsteps on the stairs stop.

"Terri?"

"No, it's me." Krista. "I'm going back to bed." Her footsteps, coming up.

"Okay." He walks down, past her door, which is closed again, arrives in the kitchen, drinks two glasses of water, takes his phone from the basket. Message from Terri. *If this is your idea of solving things, then you're truly pathetic.* OK, so you read it. *You're furious, I presume. You know, I really don't care, I'm furious too, it's petty of you, and mean, I wanted to save it. There's more love in that one conversation than there is in all of you. Fuck you. And fuck you in ancient Greek too.* Another message: *Asshole.* Her accusations are getting to be way over the top, no idea what she's on about now. He thinks about the garden of delights in his computer, brimming with available women. Available for, for … what? He thinks of coworkers who like telling him about their dating adventures, he always listens with only half an ear, a different world, but that ear is now suddenly pricked up. Maybe if he slept with someone else, if someone else liked him, maybe it would make the marriage just crumble to dust behind him, maybe he too is capable of a Terri-move; all you have to do is shift your gaze, find something new to look at, let yourself be dazzled, put off thinking about what's next, forget what you used to live for, forget what you used to deem important, just ignore the debris on your left and focus on the shiny new thing on your right instead. He opens the refrigerator, pries a few slices of salami from their plastic sleeve and opens a jar of pickles. He finishes the salami and, chomping on a pickle, pokes about in the pantry cupboard for a bag of chips or something. It suddenly occurs to him he's put himself out there rather conspicuously by posting that photo. What if someone recognized him, someone who knows Terri, someone who knows him as Krista and Ally's dad, someone from work?

When David is back in his room—she heard him walk past her door—she sneaks downstairs on her socks, opens the front door, and puts on her shoes when she's outside. It's twelve forty-five; she starts running towards the acoustic wall. She texted him at midnight saying she'd be late, but he never answered, didn't open her text either. Walking up the ramp, she slows down and lights up a Lucky Strike. He's still there, back straight as an arrow, in a djellaba, eyes closed. She puts out the cigarette and, not saying anything, sits down beside him. Without looking at her he says, "There you are." Her stomach contracts.

"Sorry, my dad just wouldn't go to bed."

"What sort of dad is he?"

"Nothing special. Just an ordinary civil servant who's divorcing my mom."

"Does he have someone else?"

"No, she does. And you?"

"My father is dead. I live with my mom and brother and two sisters. I'm the second oldest, my older brother Ali doesn't live at home anymore."

"Are you Muslim?"

"Yes."

And then, silence. For a long time. Maybe as long as half an hour. She racks her brain for something to say. Time passes. Is he bored? She turns towards him and gazes at his profile.

"Rafik."

"Krista."

Her stomach, again, in turmoil. Now he takes out his phone, searches for something on it, she gazes at his face lit from below by the screen. He's so handsome, so different from anyone she knows; and then music blasts into the silent night and he puts the phone down on the metal bench, stands up, pulls her to her feet and starts to dance. Rafik spins around, the djellaba swirls around his legs, he's got jeans on underneath. The music is Arab, she doesn't know it, she's dancing too, or a bit anyway, she wiggles her hips from side to side. It's all very weird. She can't tell Tirza. She can't tell anyone, just Ally maybe. When the song ends, he turns off the music.

"Shall I take you home?"

"Just to the corner, I guess." He walks slowly down the ramp. At the end of the street he takes both of her hands in his. In the light of the lamppost they gaze at each other. He says sleep tight, he puts his hand on his chest and bows his head. Then he turns and walks away.

She turns the corner, maybe he didn't kiss her because he's put off by her smoking? Oh God, the blood rushes to her cheeks. Are Muslims even allowed to smoke? She's about to walk on when she sees her mother, in the middle of the night, her mother with both hands pressed against the door stretching her calves. Krista stays on the other side of the street, in shadow, half-concealed by the parked cars, and stares at her. *I want you here on your knees with my prick in your mouth.* She's ruined everything. Everything. And that's the moment Krista decides she's never talking to her mother again.

She opens her front door—or actually, it's not her front door any more, strictly speaking—and steps inside. The light in the kitchen is on; no one has cleared the table. Her face is sticky with sweat and tears; she washes her face at the grimy sink, she's not going to clean up, she's the one who did the cooking tonight. She hopes the quilt is still down here, so that she can sleep on the couch without anyone noticing. Lucas's disappearance from her cellphone threw her into a state of panic. All a dream ... Light-headed from her cigarette, she felt compelled to go back to his place to make sure he still existed, that they were still an item, a possibility, a motive for burning her bridges. And to get his number, so that she could input it in her phone again. She pedaled across the bridge, feeling insecure, she should have washed her hair, she should have changed her clothes. She didn't feel strong, but that's how she *wanted* to feel, she wanted to be weak, she wanted him to tell her what to do, she who always tells everyone else what to do. She turned into his street, she rang the bell, she has a key but never uses it. She wanted him to take care of her, to be kind to her, to pat her head and run a shower for her and carry her to his bed and be tender, take his time, make love to her the way you make love when you're overcome with love.

"Wow," he said upon opening the door and looking her up and down, "that was fast." He backed away and she stepped across the threshold and softly closed the door and went into the living room, where he was standing with his back against the table, unzipping his pants. It was the first time she'd thought, He's gross. But there was something inside her that decided she deserved his vileness, that she had to submit to it. It's a punishment, punishment for walking out on her family, punishment for following her own lustful cravings, punishment for the many years she neglected those same cravings, punishment for the fact that those cravings even exist inside her, a hidden sense of unworthiness that's acknowledged, satisfied and confirmed when she allows herself to be used, like this, here, the way he wants. She was never willing to give David blowjobs, she no longer knows why, it just turned her off. Lucas showed her his dick as if it were some kind of treasure. How simple the world would be if you were always right, how smooth life would be if the only thing you desired was order and control, if you could have sex without its unpalatable aspects, and you were able to overlook the lust for power or whorishness in yourself or your partner. What she wanted was for him to caress her, to be sweet and kind, tender and paternal, that was what she'd come for, not this, but okay, this then, what the hell. What was he thinking when he looked down and saw her doing her best to satisfy him, while also doing her best not to think about what it looked like? Forty-five, she thought, Jesus Christ!

The quilt isn't down here anymore, there's just the moth-eaten blanket David refuses to get rid of and which fills her with revulsion, David's blanket, as if it's David himself that she's draping over her. But it's cold, she needs that blanket. She wraps a soft scarf around the overstuffed pillow in its ribbed case, then pulls her winter coat over her, and then the blanket. She should cancel the trip to Wassenaar, but how? Her mother's eightieth birthday. Her parents have always been so fond of David. He's at his best when he's with them, he talks books with her mother, technology with her father, acts like a man of the world, fixes things around the house. How is she going to tell them? To their ears, "fallen in love" sounds like a foolish fancy, like something against which you marshal your self-control, not something for which you abandon your family. "Fallen in love" sounds like "lost your mind." What if it *is* love? She hears a noise in the hall, the front door, a scraping sound, it's almost two o'clock, an intruder? Terri gets up from the couch and creeps upstairs, where's her phone, what can she find in the kitchen to hit him with? Standing in the stairwell, hidden in the dark, she sees her eldest daughter come in, she's already taken off her shoes, thick curls kissed by the light coming in from outside. Very slowly she shuts the door from the little hall to the kitchen, hunched over the latch, trying not to make a sound. My child, thinks Terri, and then, amazed: how can that be *my* child, that plump, curly-haired, obstinate adolescent, the first tiny baby she ever held in her arms? Once you stop taking the life you have for granted, every choice you ever made, every version of yourself, starts to feel strange. She's so exhausted. Tomorrow. She stares at Krista's stocking feet disappearing up the stairs.

After the blowjob in the living room, they showered together. Lucas puffed out his chest, stretched, and shook his hair in an intimidating show of vigor, of detachment. She wanted to stay in the shower forever, to dissolve in the water and vanish down the drain. She told him that David had deleted him from her phone. It made Lucas laugh. He grabbed a towel and stepped out. She closed her eyes and let the water run down her face.

"Send me your number again, and will you please send me all our texts again, so I don't lose them?"

"What did you say?" He had already left the bathroom. He was dressed, shoes and all, before she'd toweled herself dry. She felt very naked.

"If I can have your phone number."

He laughed again and started brushing his teeth.

"I have to go, I've got another appointment," he said.

"Yes. I have to get home."

"Whose? Isn't it supposed to be his weekend?"

"Yes."

"So?"

"Never mind. I have to go home. I don't feel well."

How unfair it is, what poles apart they are: he in his spacious, spotless life where he is gallantly making room for her, effortlessly and seemingly without any real need, and she with all her baggage and all her need, her craving for him. On Monday she's picking up the key to her apartment, Monday she'll be free at last. If only she could have waited until Ally turned eighteen, or until her parents were dead! She crawls back under the blanket and under her coat, hugging herself. Not a good person, she thinks, and then falls asleep.

SPRING

You still there?

Ally hits a tennis ball against the wall. It's drizzling but she doesn't care. Viktor came up to her today in gym and asked, "Hey, Ally, so, if you didn't have any feet, right?" She was supposed to nod, so that he could go on; he demanded it of her. She felt herself go all empty inside. She nodded. Viktor cocked his head to the side. "Would you still need shoes?" She didn't know what she was supposed to say then; a little gang of his followers had come up behind him, grinning at her. No, she said, but then Viktor lifted up his T-shirt and she realized he was wearing her bra. "What've you got *this* for, then?" An explosion of noise, laughter. Then they ran off. She automatically put her hands on the small breasts hiding under her gym shirt, still new and unfamiliar to her, and bound for an as-yet-unknown final dimension. When the gym teacher wasn't looking Viktor would lift up his shirt, jeering, "Look, even if you don't have any tits!" Gym ended, in the locker room she picked up her clothes, which were scattered all over the floor, stuffed everything back into her gym bag, showered with her back to the others, and got dressed, without her bra; nobody said anything to her. Leo wasn't there that day. At lunch she sat with Bobby on the low wall in the corner of the playground, and they talked about other things—*Minecraft*, Percy Jackson, the best way to make grilled cheese: in a frying pan, according to Bobby.

After school there was nobody home. She had a cup of tea and a couple of cookies. She did her homework, she stared at the empty spaces in the house, her mother's clothes gone from the closet, half-empty shelves in the bookcases, she leafed through the picture albums of her birth and David and Terri's wedding and Krista's birth, the family before she existed. When they used to look at them together, lying on their stomachs on the rug, Krista would say, "It was such a happy time, just the three of us, the happiest time of our lives." It made Ally cry sometimes, even though she knew Krista was only joking. She ate a couple more cookies, put the albums back, and deleted the class chat without reading the comments. Then she took her racket and went outside. Isabel was there in the square with another girl, their boobs clearly visible under their jackets. They left soon after. Isabel waved. Ally yelled "Bye!" Now she's hitting the ball against the wall, she is trying not to think about anything, just the ball, just her hand, just the wall, the gray spot on the wall that's her target, about Marina Flakovitz, who might walk by, recognize Ally's talent, and whisk her off to England, where they'd speak English and play tennis all day long.

"Ally!" Her dad is straddling his bike, his foot on the curb. She runs up to him, but when she's halfway there she remembers she's twelve and isn't supposed to throw herself into his arms.

"Hello, my little girl. Everything good?"

"Yeah."

"At school?"

"Yeah."

"Nothing special?"

"No."

"Let's decide you can't say yes or no, all right?"

"Okay, fine."

"What should we have for dinner?"

"Dunno. Stamppot?"

"Endive?" She nods. "Coming?" He swings his leg over the saddle and pulls his bicycle up on the sidewalk.

Propped against the vase on the table there's an envelope with Krista's name on it. Terri's handwriting. David places it in front of her.

"Yeah."

"Had you seen it?"

"Yeah."

"Aren't you going to open it?"

"Yeah. Later."

David starts to peel the potatoes. Ally is leaning over a textbook, her sleek hair falling like a curtain around her. Krista is playing with her phone. David reads a text from S. *Are you still there?* Later, he thinks. *Yes*, he writes. He puts the potatoes on to boil and washes and minces the endive, he slices a red onion and cuts cheese into little cubes, opens a bottle of Riesling and pours himself a glass. The situation can be termed peaceful; peace has started to return to their home, Terri is gone and the more distant she is, the greater the sense of tranquility, her letter on the table the only thing to disturb it. As if she's thinking the same thing, Krista, in an abrupt move, suddenly tears it open and starts to read. Ally peeks at her out of the corner of her eye. David glances sideways at her face. It's set in a frown. After a while she folds the paper again and lets it fall on the table. She stares out the window, her hands folded on top of the letter. She almost doesn't look like a child, he thinks, like this, in this pose. He finishes his glass, holds his breath. No one speaks. No one does anything.

He fills their glasses with iced tea. He

mashes the potatoes and stirs them to a creamy consistency with butter and hot milk. Krista is intent on her phone, as usual. There's music coming from it, something Arabic, she glances at her father who is looking at her, who would love to know what the letter said and is now listening, with a cocked head and the tea towel slung over his shoulder.

"Like it?" she asks.

"Yes. Sure. What is it?"

She shrugs. "Moroccan." He sets the other side of the table. The girls pull up their chairs. He stirs the endive, cheese and onion into the mash. "Voilà," he says, setting down the pan in front of them.

Krista takes a bite. After two weeks' radio silence, Rafik sent her the music they'd danced to. She nearly went berserk when she got it. She'd thought she must have done something very wrong; three days after their encounter she'd sent him a message. After a great deal of hemming and hawing, she'd opted for a photo of the lamppost where they'd said goodbye. When he didn't respond, she'd started feeling horribly embarrassed about that picture, what a lame idea that was! She kept staring at that corny lamppost, you couldn't even tell it was the right one, you could hardly even tell what it was supposed to be. Was he insulted? Or had he already deleted her from his phone and from his thoughts? She'd seen him again only once, he'd been with his pals; he'd nodded, and looked very serious and a little somber. She'd smiled back at him. Maybe she'd looked kind of dumb; afterwards she'd recorded herself by propping her cell up on the piano, smiling the way she'd smiled—recorded it because in the mirror you only see your mirror image and that's a completely different version of the real thing, and yes, maybe it did look kind of dumb, smiling like that. The next time she saw him, she'd show him how serious she could be too. She tried to think of something to send him, something to cancel out the lamppost, something that would quell his disdain, that might break the silence. This afternoon, tired of endlessly hunting for the right emoji or the right words, she'd sent him a very simple, *Hi Rafik, you still there?* And then, right away, he'd sent her that song. *Hi Krista, here I am. Rafik.* Just now she texted him asking if they could meet again some time. That act of daring propelled her to open Terri's letter. If she had the guts to send Rafik that message, surely she had the guts to read the letter. Terri has moved into her new apartment, and she wants Ally and Krista to stay with her part of the week. When Terri came over to discuss it with the three of them the day before yesterday, Krista hadn't come home. After seven texts from Terri and ten phone calls, she'd blocked her mother's number. She hadn't returned home that night until just before midnight. David had waited up for her in the kitchen and made her a cup of cocoa. He'd looked so pathetically sad. Terri was out to turn him into a complete wreck, it seemed to her. That's what she'd told him, and he'd denied it. He'd stuck up for Terri. He told her Terri needed space, and it didn't mean she didn't love them anymore. She doesn't love *me* anymore, he said, but she still loves you two deeply. Krista said she would never set foot in that apartment. Why should she, she lived *here*, she was fifteen, she wasn't going to let herself get pushed around, shunted back and forth by someone having a midlife crisis. She thought of the revolting text exchange between her mother and her boyfriend, she had only to think of that, she had only to think of her mother's mouth, of the way the dude wrote about her body, and her mom's slavish response, to stick to her decision.

"Would you like another helping, Kris?"

"No thanks, Dad."

"Ally?"

"Sure."

"Is it true Terri didn't really want to have children originally?"

"Where did you get that idea, is that what she wrote?"

"No."

"Oh."

They had waited ten years. She was the one who wanted children. Not having them would have been fine with him too. He can't for the life of him remember how the decision came about. But he does know that it was her, *she* was the one, for cripes' sake, and he'll remind her too sometime, who'd pushed for it. She wanted to have kids, she wanted to get married, she wanted a house in the suburbs, she wanted all the things she's now blaming him for, all the things she's now claiming he somehow ensnared her with, as if they were never her things at all, but are just proof of how dull and bourgeois *he* is. Children are one of those rare things in life you can't change your mind about, and family is part of that equation. She could have asked for an open marriage, he is more and more certain he could have dealt with that, especially now that he's started talking to that woman he met on the dating site, the woman who signs her emails with *S*; now that he finds himself (strangely enough— for what is it really but an intense dialogue with a complete stranger?) in a state of constant erotic alertness. He is suddenly aware of women he sees in the street, he'll suddenly see a colleague and fantasize about her touching him, he daydreams about S although he doesn't even know what she looks like, but she must have boobs, and a mouth, and ...

"But? So?"

"So—what?"

"Didn't Terri want us?"

"What gave you *that* idea, she wanted you very much, just as I did, we wanted you desperately."

"Okay."

Why couldn't she just have had an affair in secret, lots of people do it, some even manage to save their marriage that way. Why blow it all up? He thinks of S. He should be thinking about S. It's the best distraction he's had in weeks. They write to each other dozens of times a day.

Why hasn't she called it off?

He presses bits of crumbly dough into the tart tin, pinching and patting it into a whole. Less satisfying than rolling it into a circle of even thinness, but doing it this way may make for a tastier crust, he read that somewhere, and the uneven surface left by his fingers won't be noticed under the filling. He is fattening up both Ally and himself, he cooks and roasts, fries and bakes, he whips cream, creams butter and sugar together, glazes, flambés, deep-fries, purees. He reads recipes, tries out new things. The activity soothes him, the creamy textures and crispy crusts and all the sweet and savory intensities comfort him. Even Krista has begun eating again, though he can't seem to persuade Terri that that's good news—that it's too bad she's snubbing her mother, but that the simple fact she's eating again is at least something to be happy about. Terri is capable of seeing only one thing about Krista, and that is her refusal to talk to her. She calls Kris by turns childish, recalcitrant, manipulative, insubordinate, vindictive, and impossible. It makes him feel hopeless, why can't Terri see that Krista is unhappy and what she needs isn't criticism, but love? He shakes his head, he seems to go through life shaking his head these days. Oh God, he thinks as he arranges the peach segments on the dough in an overlapping pattern (concentrating on the tart, it had clean slipped his mind for a few minutes), I have a date with a woman, another woman, a woman other than my wife, a woman I don't know—and yet he does, since they've been exchanging both intimate and heartfelt messages. He folds the edges of the dough into a plump brim, brushes it with egg wash and slides the tart into the oven. Then he finds himself grabbing the counter like a seasick passenger hanging on to a ship's railing in a storm. What was I thinking, thinks David, who do I think I am, I wouldn't know what to do, or if the way we did it is the way you're supposed to do it. Krista walks into the kitchen, followed by Luna and Tirza. The tart is for the girls to share, and tonight he'll leave them money for pizza, when all's said and done they like takeout pizza better than anything he rustles up in his kitchen. She's the one who suggested it; she doesn't want a relationship, she says, but a lover; she wrote, *Make love to me the way you write to me.* And that's how they arrived at their plan: she would wait for him in bed, with the front door unlatched.

"Dad."

"What?"

"What are you doing?"

"How do you mean?"

"You're making weird noises."

"What?" See, he's losing control. Get a grip. "What kind of noises?"

"Uh … like a … seal?" The girls are giggling

at different pitches, like a chorus of background singers. *Make love to me the way you write to me.* What does that even mean? Why hasn't she called it off? What kind of woman leaves her door unlatched to let a strange man into her house? Krista and her friends disappear upstairs. What if he gets paralyzed with fear? He starts loading the dishwasher. Wipes the counter and sink clean. Ally stares at him with her racket in her hand. Is her life falling apart? Is this what they call drama? The room smells of pie in the oven. Obsessive baking can be added to the list of her father's weird behaviors. On top of the drinking, secret weeping, heading out to the office ridiculously early and coming home ridiculously early in the afternoon. Yesterday she went to Terri's new house. Terri tried to get her to tell her whether David was working on getting Krista to forgive her and get in touch with her again. Ally felt torn. What was she supposed to say? What should she tell, what should she keep to herself, when is it a betrayal, what rights does a person have who's moved to a house on the other side of a river? She tried to stay noncommittal. Afterwards Terri helped her with her homework. Ally didn't have the nerve to tell her she didn't need any help. The new home has turned her mother into someone to be polite to. If Ally acted sulky and refused to accept her help, Terri would be all lonely in that strange, empty house.

"Don't you want any furniture?"

"But I have furniture, can't you see?"

"Don't you want pictures and stuff?"

"But I do have stuff! I bought you a bed."

"I'd rather sleep at home."

"Okay. That's fine. You'll stay for dinner, though, won't you?"

"What are we having?"

"Does it matter?" Yes.

"Not really."

"Lentils and vegetables."

"Yum." As if they were in a different country, with different rules and customs.

"It's healthy, anyway. Has Krista started eating again?"

"Yeah."

"Really?"

"Daddy bakes pies almost every day."

"Really?"

As if she'd betrayed him after all ... The lentils were yucky but she finished her plate and said she liked it. Terri said her friend would never come here, that the house was meant just for her and Krista and Ally. She said it as if Ally had asked about it and she was now reluctantly telling her. Why didn't she just introduce him to her? Was Terri ashamed of her daughters, of her? Ally tried to think of an inoffensive topic, something fun to tell her about. In the end she said she'd learned how to put a spin on her serve, which wasn't true, she's known how to for ages, but she's improved a lot recently. Terri wasn't really listening.

"You could also bring one of your friends. Why don't you bring Isabel for a sleepover next weekend?"

"I'm not friends with Isabel anymore."

"Or someone else."

It took fourteen minutes to ride home. David wanted her to sleep over at Terri's tonight, it would be easier for him, because he has a party to go to and is worried she'll be scared home alone. She shouldn't tell him she's scared anymore. She has to accept that it isn't worth the risk. First of all, there's the risk that her father, if he can't go to parties or conferences anymore, will feel just as trapped as Terri did, and walk out on them too. That's what she heard, with her head in the stairwell and her cheek on the coir runner: Terri literally telling him she wasn't an individual anymore, that she couldn't go to the parties or conferences she wanted, that she'd had to give up a whole part of herself for the family. It was clear she had to give her parents space, space to be more than just parents. And the other risk is being forced to sleep at Terri's. And that's much scarier than being home alone.

"Hey, Allybel. How you doin'? I'm not home this evening, you know that, don't you?"

"Yes."

"Okay?"

"Yes."

"I'm going to a party. It may get late."

"It's fine, Dad."

"Krista's staying home; she promised. Tirza and Luna are here too."

"No problem, Daddy. Just going up to my room now."

"I baked a peach tart."

"I can smell it. Yummy."

"Just an experiment!"

"Okay."

"In an hour."

"All right, Dad." It worked, she even manages a grin at Krista on the landing, her tears stay inside until she's in her room. She cries silently, her cheek pressed into her blanket, she thinks about Marina Flakovitz, that Marina's standing behind her with her arm around her, with her hard soft warm ripped body cupping hers, that she's showing Ally how to hit the ball the way she does.

Downstairs David is studying S's email again.

When you ring the bell. I'll open the door downstairs and get into bed. You'll take the elevator to the seventh floor. Once there, turn right, around the corner, I'll leave my door open a crack. You'll come in and shut the door. The bathroom is to your left. The kitchen on your right. Maybe you'll feel like having a glass of water. Maybe you'll want to have a look around, to get a better sense of me, your first visual cues as to who I am. To the left of the bathroom is the living room. I think it would be a bit mad but also great fun if you decided to play something on the piano that's in there. Your profile says you know how to play, but we've never discussed it. Next to the piano you'll see a door, you'll find yourself walking through a closet as if through a floodgate: on the far side is another door, both will be open, don't worry, it's not complicated. My bedroom will be in darkness; wait until your eyes get used to the dark and you can make out my bed against the far wall, so you can gauge the distance. Then you'll close the door behind you. You'll lie down next to me. I'll put my arms around you. I'll wrap my legs around you. S.

Defiled

"Oh! Take a right here, I know a terrific place for a swim."

They're returning from a visit to her sister's; it's unusually hot for April. Lucas hadn't wanted to come at first, but it was important to her, and he decided to humor her. He thinks: This is where it starts, the bending and stretching for the sake of another, stretching yourself until with all the pulling and pleating all the elasticity is lost. Some people are made of a more forgiving sort of material, he just isn't, could that be it?

"Here?" He resists the urge to keep going straight instead, and turns right. The road winds slowly down, she points out another turnoff, and he swings the car into it. The asphalt turns into a dirt road. He glances sideways, she nods, promises him it'll be fun. He turns his head back to the road, which is plastering his car with dust.

"We should park here, I think, oh, maybe not," says Terri. He was already slowing down. "A little farther, uh ..." She's peering out the window. "It's changed quite a bit. Yes, here!"

"Here?" He brakes.

"No, over there!"

He steps on the gas again, then stops the car. Exhales through his teeth, slowly. They get out, set off down a path and are soon standing on the banks of the lake. She starts to take off her clothes. There's not a soul around, she's right, it's a nice spot, a secret spot, and just as he's thinking that, the smell of fried food assaults his nose. His feet sink up to his ankles in mud. They lower themselves in as quickly as they can, swim away from the mucky bottom, around a stand of weeds, only to come upon the sight of a little beach crowded with people. Secret spot—like hell!

"That was never here before!" She swims out ahead of him, she's laughing, she doesn't care. The water is cold. He forgets the mud and the dust on his car and dives down and grabs her feet. She splashes free and with one smooth breaststroke swims out of reach. He thinks of Femke, whom he occasionally sees on television these days. He's always startled to see it. Femke is the most emotionally inaccessible woman he's ever had; she was scared to death, and her denial of that fact was part and parcel of it. It was his fault, she would say, she wasn't unresponsive, it was he who wasn't sensitive enough, or she didn't feel safe with him or something. He called her his little border guard, she was constantly monitoring the boundaries between them. They'd been looking for a house when he got cold feet. Who's the one afraid of intimacy now? she'd asked. Since then she's published a whole stack of articles and a book on the subject. He floats on his back and gazes up at the sky. He doesn't read her stuff anymore, on a professional level he considers it trivial; still, there *is* something to it, there's something about intimacy and romantic relationships, they're always turning up in each other's orbit.

"What are you grinning about?"

"I'm floating."

"You're grinning while floating."

"I was thinking of Femke, an ex-girlfriend."

"How long ago?"

"Half a lifetime."

"How long were you together?"

"Four years, about."

"I see!"

"My longest relationship."

"Good for you, well done!"

Keeping his eyes closed he grabs her wrist just as she's about to push him under. He twists up and dunks her, immediately pulling her back up. She yells. "No, *this* is well done," he says, "seeing you with my eyes shut, knowing exactly what you're about to do." He bites her hand softly. "Come on, let's get out over there on the beach, to avoid the muck back there."

They swim around the small green outcropping and wade onto dry land. As blindly as they're able, they thread their way through the beach towels littered with people, their belongings and their picnics, through the fast-food smell wafting from a French fries stand, naked but pretending not to be.

They shake themselves dry like dogs and let their clothes do the rest, then drive back to the city.

"There never used to be any people there, I swear."

"Do you want to get something to eat?"

"Okay. Lucas?"

"Yeah."

"Tell me about that longest relationship of yours, with Femke, what it was like."

"It was as these things go: fun at first, then it gradually grew less interesting, and she wanted things I didn't want, and I wanted things she didn't want, and it lost its whole point."

"Did you mind that?"

"It was no longer fun."

"Because it has to be fun."

"I think so, yes."

"But what if it's hard?"

"Yes?"

"Isn't that by definition no fun?"

"It doesn't have to be, I'm assuming."

"Because?"

"Because what?"

"You give me so little to go on."

"What do you want to know?"

"I want to get to know you."

"Here I am."

"You ask me things too."

"Is that so?"

"About what sex is like with David."

"Is like?"

"Was like."

"Do I?"

"You have."

"With Femke I had sex the way you have sex when you're twenty." Her head jerks sharply aside, it's her weak spot, he knows it. "A lot of excitement, not much refinement. I don't know, we were kind of boring as a couple, I think, in bed too. A handsome couple. But boring."

"So? Was she very pretty?"

"She was very pretty, as was I." He grins at

her. She smacks him on the arm. "Watch out, I'm driving!"

"Prettier than me?"

"She was twenty-five years younger, for a start. Back then, anyway."

"So was I, back then."

He parks the car in front of Da Augusto and turns to face her. Her hair is wet, her eyes are bright. "We're ordering osso buco, girl." Women like being called girl.

"Do you ever see her now?"

"Yes, as do you." He tells her the woman's full name.

"Oh, really? The expert on romantic love!"

"It's all theory." Lucas holds the door open for her, he is greeted as the regular customer he is, they sit down at a tiny table by the window. It's all good, Terri thinks, as long as she's able to see the two of them, her life, through the lens of her feelings for Lucas, it's all good. It's a question of discipline.

"I'm so glad you came with me, now my sister knows what I'm talking about when I mention you. That's nice for me. I'll spare you my parents for now. What did you think of her?"

"She doesn't look like you."

"No, she doesn't."

"Do you want wine?" He orders a glass for her, and then one for himself.

"Why did you order two different wines?"

"Because we're two different people."

"What's the difference?"

"I can't even begin to describe it."

"Try."

"No."

"Lotte is important to me, but when I left David, something between the two of us changed. She denies it, but I think she disapproves. Our parents are still together, and she's still with her husband. That said, she's only been with him ten years."

"Only ten years?" The wine arrives. She looks at his glass. "No, you can't have a sip."

"Why not?"

"It's my wine. And that's your wine."

She laughs. "Haven't you ever wanted that? Something that's forever?" She lifts her glass at him, and takes a sip.

"Well?"

"Yes, very nice, delicious."

"No."

"No what?"

"To your question."

"Oh. And how long do you give *us*?"

"What? How do you mean?"

The waiter brings them side plates of salad. A basket of fluffy white bread with a salted crust. He won't be drawn into a conversation about Lotte and her parents, or about him and his past relationships, or about the two of them and the future in any serious way, that's clear, it simply doesn't interest him, and suddenly she's sorry; with David they always discussed other people, they'd try to figure them out, anyway, and would help each other do so.

"Are you ever in touch with Femke anymore?"

"Are you jealous?"

"Not at all; just curious."

"No. Never."

"What do you want, Lucas?"

"I want you to drink a glass of wine or two and enjoy your fennel salad and the osso buco, and then come home with me and take your clothes off and put on what I've bought you, and ..." And so Lucas's words turn her head misty, and her body ready for action.

So there they are, sitting at the little table by the window, bathed in warm indoor light while outside it's growing dark, with wine in their glasses and food on their plates. Terri who, by taking Lucas to the secret swimming spot of young-and-in-love Terri and young-and-in-love David, has just managed to defile it, Terri who isn't thinking about her children anymore, who doesn't particularly care that Lucas never asks after them, who ignores the fact that for him it's a problem that she has children, an affliction—the parenthood disease. As long she keeps riding this wave, everything's great, they're a handsome, sophisticated couple, footloose and fancy-free, not poor, not sick, and not trapped in some monotonous semi-existence. Later they'll have sex, and it will excite Terri that he makes love to her without even a trace of tenderness.

Not even three hundred feet from Da Augusto, David is on his way to his rendezvous with

Sev, excited, nervous, don't walk too fast, don't get all sweaty. The city is looking lovely with dusk falling, draining color from the world. Back home, Krista and her friends talk about boys. Krista giggles a bit at the mention of Gijs, a boy in their class; she's keeping Rafik to herself. Ally is in her own bedroom, her eyes are red and puffy from crying, she's better off staying in her room for the time being. She takes out her diary but can't think what to write, it's all too awful, or too confusing, or just too much. She has no idea where to start.

Fata morgana

His silhouette fills the doorframe. He is big, tall. He stays there for a moment, as per her instructions, to get used to the darkness of her bedroom; she can hear him breathe. He bends down to untie his shoelaces, he unclasps his belt and takes off his pants, he unbuttons his shirt, she can't see much, it's too dark, but from the sounds and the vague outline of the movements she can work out what's happening; she flings aside the covers to let him in, he sits down, she feels the warmth of his body, she smells his smell; he gets under the covers beside her a bit brusquely. She slips her arm behind his head and shoulders and along his neck, he presses his face into her throat, then to her chest, she puts her other arm around him, she slings a leg around him, they lie there, they breathe, they just lie there and breathe. He smells good, thank God. They've been corresponding for four weeks, sometimes as many as forty texts a day, she wrote to him about the article she's working on, on the national security policy's effects on public safety; he was able to relate it to his own life, told her how to his wife, security had taken a backseat to the lack of freedom it entails. They were candid with each other; he wrote that he wasn't ready for a relationship, she wrote that she wasn't looking for one either, he made her laugh; he told her frankly that he was unhappy; they were open with each other, every message drew them closer. And now he's here, the unhappy man; she gently butts his head backward so that she can reach his lips. What is love but deciding that you are ready for it, and then finding an object upon which to project your desires? She kisses him, they kiss, gently, he slips his hand under her nightshirt down her back, his hand is warm, her skin is smooth, he tastes good, thank God, his mouth is warm and wet and she's relieved to see a person's physical appearance can match his words. She nestles her hand in his neck, slick with sweat, she feels his hair, dense hair, she feels his ear, a modest ear, close to his head, small earlobe, his hand has traveled all the way down her back and he rests his hand on her bottom, she feels the heat of his hand. They kiss, their hands are still for a while, then start moving again. Her hand on his flank; he sucks in his stomach. She pushes him gently onto his back and climbs on top of him, she folds herself around him, clamps her legs around his hips. For a while they just lie there like that, their bodies sinking into each other. She thinks of Erich Fromm, who calls love a fata morgana, a mirage in a desert of loneliness, she thinks of films in which people move from kissing to fucking within thirty seconds as if it's the most normal thing in the world, where neither clumsiness nor syncopated movement ever slow the proceedings down, she thinks of Johan, the last man in her bed, the familiarity, she thinks how interchangeable men are, whether that is true, who she is, where she is. She is here, she thinks, with the man who told her about his pain, who zoomed in on her in the chat room, whose prick she feels between her legs, but whose face she has yet to see.

She lights a candle next to the bed.

"Let's start slow," she whispers, meaning the dim candlelight, then turns and looks at him. Her hair is dark, her face is warm, that much he can see, her look is tender and she has bags under her eyes, she's smiling, she's exactly the way he expected, even though he had no expectations and only realizes it now.

"Hello ma'am," he whispers, "I'm David."

"Hello David, I'm Sev. Christ! You have an Amsterdam accent!" She laughs. He wept, just now, when they were fucking, she wiped the tears from his face and simply continued. That was nice, the fact that she didn't see him as a wreck, that she understood the consolation lay in her acceptance of his tears, and in not attaching too much significance to them. He doesn't know why he wept, it may just have been because someone had wrapped her arms around him and wanted him. He laughs too. Sev starts telling him about a movie, a Dutch movie, she doesn't remember the title, in which a woman and a man meet at the ice rink, ride home never exchanging a word, park their bikes outside her house, go in, make love, and then when it's over he finally says something, she doesn't remember what exactly, upon which the woman exclaims, "Oh, God, a Belgian!"

"I don't think I have such a strong Amsterdam accent."

"No, but you can definitely hear it." She hands him a glass of water. "Or would you like some wine?"

"Yes please."

She gets out of bed, shrugs on a long shirt, or maybe it's a dress, or something in between; is he supposed to get out of bed and go after her?

"Back in a jiffy."

So, no. He looks around the room, there's a family portrait, the woman left of center may be Sev, he isn't certain, he's only seen her once, and then only a glimpse, by candlelight. In a corner stands a chair with a stack of books on it. He can taste dust in his mouth and nose, he's oversensitive in that regard. He puts his shirt back on, he piles the pillows up against the wall and sits down. To think he had the guts to do this! he congratulates himself, and what now? Is he supposed to do something now? The only other occasion in his life that he went to bed with someone for the first time, it marked the beginning of a whole life, but this time he already has a whole life, even if it doesn't feel at all whole in the other sense of the word.

SUMMER

Abyss

Getting to know another person brings with it a sense of awe—here's a whole other being, with a whole life of their own, a history separate from yours, a mystery opening up before you, a prospect unfolding; you start off cautiously, you try to hide what's less admirable about yourself, you try not to be too direct, you dance about, looking for ways to dodge the absolute truth, you cajole the other into doing what you want. In that dance you do your very best not to step on the other's toes, because that would reveal what a boor you are, and could mean the end. But then, eventually, there comes a turning point—I see the same thing happening all around me—when you're no longer dancing but heading straight for your goal, you relax and, relaxing, no longer hide the things you hid before, and when you do step on your partner's toes, you just decide that foot was terribly in the way. You start interfering in each other's habits, you start teaching each other where to put your feet, what to eat or wear or say, you coordinate your tastes and your bedtimes, you start feeling responsible for their behavior in public. You finish each other's sentences; you complement one another. You think of the other person as a part of yourself. You misbehave in front of them as you would misbehave in private, and they do the same, and you forgive each other for it, and so that's how you really get to know one another, the entire person, you believe, but if you're honest you know that's not true, there are things you don't tell, nasty thoughts about your partner, tempting thoughts about third parties, insights into yourself, fantasies about a different life. In fact, you're giving the other person only half of yourself, and don't even want to get to know the rest of who they are, because that wouldn't square with the fairy tale you've talked yourself into. You jealously guard a small oasis inside you, which fills up with freedom or loneliness or a combination of the two. You no longer want to get to know the other person, you just recognize them now, again and again, the energy you'd mobilized to understand who he or she really is has been idled, and you are now directing that energy out at the world again, or into your work, or into your kids. You're no longer looking at each other; you're both looking out instead. You've lost your distance from one another, you're losing your perspective on each other, you're losing respect for each other, and a new distance starts to grow up between you, but now the distance is of a different order, there's no open space left in which to meet, there are rules and ingrained habits in the way, laws and expectations everywhere. The distance turns into an abyss, it's a secret, or it's the emptiness in you the other hasn't been able to fill. It's a ravine, a deep hole you either ignore or find yourselves endlessly attempting to plug with promises, reassurances, turf wars, second thoughts, or secret addictions. Don't ask me what that looks like, the abyss as a jagged wound running through the joint terrain, ringed with the hills and the valleys, earthly delights beneath the pergola, secret

gardens, lagoons, and no one knows how deep.
That land, the country that is love, and the way
the seasons follow one another, the way the land-
scape changes depending on the conditions, tor-
rential rain, scorching heat or an earthquake ...
I've never been very good at it, I'd always be the
one jumping into the abyss in no time.

They are all finally asleep. Sev, working late
and ruminating about Tolstoy, about the
happiness of families, about David and his
so-called disaster, and about her own inepti-
tude for commitment. David, who stopped
brooding and proceeded to jerk off instead,
fantasizing about Sev watching him do it.
Ally, tossing and turning, trapped in nebu-
lous nightmares just not terrifying enough
to wake her. And Krista and Terri and Lucas,
because it's late, and because they're exhausted.

And before they rise and shine again, the
city wakes up for what will prove to be another scorcher. There's a watering ban on,
and the city's gardens and parks are wilting.
Another day of no rain. Before even getting

out of bed, Ally is already fretting about climate change. Krista, on the other side of the wall, has received a text from Rafik; heart pounding, she runs it through Google Translate, then softly mouths the clumsy verses it delivers, under the covers. David brushes his teeth in the shower and thinks about his work and what else can go wrong in his life, but this afternoon he's going over to Sev's again, and all he needs to do is tell Sev it's the last time; by repeating that mantra he can circumvent his sense of duty, prevent the guilt, and wonder at the liberating, thrilling thought that he's a lover, the lover of a woman who asks nothing of him, demands nothing of him, with whom he shares nothing but the bed and his thoughts.

Terri wakes up alone, Lucas is gone and hasn't sent or left a message. Sitting at her kitchen table, she rereads her letter to Krista and eats her oats cooked in oat milk.

Sev gets up with a vague feeling of sadness. David is coming over tonight, that ought to cheer her up, but she senses that that fact and her sadness are somewhere connected, she doesn't know how. There's still a long time to go until nightfall. In the shower she rinses the sleep and the stiffness from her body. At the exact same time, unaware of this synchronicity, Sev and David both wash their hair, let the lukewarm water stream over their faces, and think about each other.

So what do you really want?

"What do you think, Terri?" Across the table, her coworker looks at her expectantly. She hasn't been listening, but it's amazing how far you can get with half an ear and some bravado. Never admit you weren't listening, never say you're sorry, just come out with some bland generalization delivered with the cool assurance of a point of view.

"It's a good idea, absolutely, but as long as the details aren't yet fully worked out, it seems to me, we can't really get the ball rolling. I propose getting it written up, and then let's reconvene here next week." While speaking, she begins stacking up the papers within reach. The others all nod. This way they can finally end this meeting and do nothing further, but with the contented feeling that a decision has been made. Everyone leaves. Terri stays behind, she checks to see if there's a message from Lucas, or from her children, or even from David. She puts her head down on the table for just a moment. In the first letter to Krista, she kept it pretty superficial. She wrote that she needed to give herself some space, and that she thought her timing would square with Krista's need to assert her independence in the world, when she wouldn't need Terri in the caretaking-mother role as much. She wrote that it was an opportunity to relate to each other as people; Terri no longer just the mother catering to her family's needs, but an individual choosing to be her own person, and as such, able to be a sounding board for her daughter in many more ways than before, because Terri is giving free rein to so many other facets of herself. And Krista would no longer be just the daughter, but also a person in her own right, taking her first steps in all kinds of new directions. It was all a bit abstract, naturally, maybe too abstract for a girl of fifteen. And seeing that in these past few months that talk has never gotten off the ground, or, indeed, that they haven't spoken at all since her letter, Terri decided to make another stab at it. Not to nag; if these months have made anything clear, it is that insistently phoning and texting, complaining, demanding a response, doesn't work. What she has to do is tempt Krista with—with what, actually?—with information, with a story, without invoking family ties, or duty of any sort, but simply trying to start a conversation by revealing some truths about herself. That's what she had in mind yesterday when she started on that second letter, and it inspired her, her own honest introspection inspired her, she wasn't doing it just for Krista, she was also doing it for herself. And it helped, somehow, to make sense of the empty, hollow feeling Krista's snubbing has given her. She would take her time, the time to do it right. She was prepared to spend a week on it, if necessary. She stopped when she couldn't think of what should come next, and because Lucas had arrived. Now that he's gone without leaving word, leaving early this morning or maybe last night, she's trying to go over what happened last night. Was there something wrong, did she do something wrong? They didn't speak much, they had sex, then she made a salad and they ate it. He read something to her, she only half listened. Then they had sex again, on the floor, leaving a big wet spot afterwards because it was hot in her apartment, and they'd both sweated buckets. She blotted it up with a towel, they showered and then went to bed, both tossing and turning for a while until she fell asleep. Did she fail to notice something? Did he say something about having to go to work early? He didn't usually make any effort to be quiet if he got up before her. Was she so fast asleep? Or did he sneak out like a thief in the night, was he leaving her? She glances at her phone again. He was online fifteen minutes ago, so it's not as if he can't send her a message. She puts her head down on the table again. She has to get to work. Maybe she should let Lucas read that letter to Krista. She dials his number.

"Hi Terri."

"Is everything all right?"

"Well, I'm at work."

"You didn't say goodbye."

"What?"

"This morning. You didn't say goodbye to me this morning."

"You were asleep."

"I was worried."

"I'm working."

"Uh-huh."

"Are you checking up on me now?"

"Uh. No. I was worried."

"I don't like that."

"Me neither, but I couldn't help it."

"I don't like you bothering me with those feelings."

"Oh?"

"It's a matter of good hygiene to keep them to yourself, Terri."

"Hygiene?"

"Yes."

"What's hygiene got to do with love?"

"I'm hanging up."

"No! You're not!"

"Oh no?"

"No, Lucas, I'm talking to you."

"Aha, well."

"Tell me what you mean."

"You can't control my feelings, you can't make me responsible for yours."

"But you are responsible for some of my feelings, or for the reason I have them, anyway. My excitement, my love, my interest in certain things, aren't those allowed either? I love you because of you."

"No, you love me because of *you*. And because I'm not David."

"Is that cynicism?"

"Who knows."

"Lucas."

"Terri."

"I was scared you'd left me."

"Aha."

"So it isn't true?"

"Would that be so bad?"

"Jesus, Lucas."

"Yeah."

"Why don't you say, 'No, it isn't true,' if it isn't true?"

"Why should I?"

"Because I'm feeling really bad."

"Ah."

"And it's easy for you to make it go away."

"Is that true?"

"Unless you did leave me, then."

"I don't like it when you dictate what I'm supposed to say."

"Just say it isn't true!" Terri hurts her hand whacking it against the edge of the table.

"Say what isn't true?"

"That it's not true that you left me, last night, or early this morning."

"Why should I do that?"

"Why not? If it isn't so? If it isn't true, can't you just ..."

"Say it, yes. Yes? Before you know it, we'll have to swear to each other we haven't left on a daily basis."

"It's the first time I've asked for that sort of ..."

"Reassurance."

"Yes!"

"And the last time."

"Hmm."

"I'm at work, Terri." He has lured her into a trap of some sort, she thinks, he's turned an absolutely normal question into a crime.

"Can I assume that you'll tell me?"

"Tell you what?"

"That you'll tell me if you *are* leaving me?"

"Sure thing."

"And if you cheat on me?"

"If I cheat on you? What are you talking about?"

"If you're unfaithful?"

"So did we agree we were going to be exclusive?"

"Didn't we?"

"Not that I know of."

"Oh."

"Terri."

"I just assumed."

"Haven't you learned a thing from your god-blasted marriage?"

"What?"

"*What*, what?"

"Are you mad at me now? No! Don't hang up."

"I don't belong to you."

"Who *do* you belong to then? And weren't you ever going to tell me?"

"Did we ever agree to do that?"

"I should think it's pretty obvious."

"Maybe you should start at the beginning next time."

"At what beginning, Lucas?"

"At what kind of relationship I might want to have with you. At telling me your expectations. Before taking for granted ..."

"Maybe we should be doing this face to face."

"Oh yeah?"

"I'd much rather, then we could ..."

"Do you want our relationship to become a drag? Are we going to start mollycoddling each other, needing constant reassurance, imposing restrictions and obligations?"

"No, of course I don't want that."

"Do you really need me to justify myself, if I feel like going home early and getting to work?"

"I don't see that as having to justify yourself."

"What is it then?"

"Communication? Involving each other in the conversation."

"The same lame conversation millions of other couples are having, you mean?"

"Hmm."

"Do you want us to grow old together too?"

"Excuse me?"

"Are there any other clichés you can't rise above?"

"So what do you really want, then?"

"What do I really want …"

"From me. Yes."

"Oh." Silence. "I like going to bed with you." Silence. "Are you still there?"

"You're not being very nice."

"Do you really want another nice guy?"

"Well, no, but …"

"Listen, Terri."

"Yes?"

"You are not the only interesting woman in the world. You're not the only beautiful woman in the world either. And you're not the only woman in the world who's in love."

Now she clams up, and after a silence of at least twenty seconds he hangs up. He slams his phone down on the sofa and, planting his fists on the table, hangs his head. He had a restless night, and finally decided to get up at about six in the morning. Terri was quiet and somber last night, fretting about her contact with her daughters, moaning about divorce being harder than she thought, about that prick husband of hers refusing to cooperate. He didn't feel like getting involved, he didn't feel like consoling her. She's beautiful, but there are plenty of beautiful women out there. She's interesting, but there are plenty of interesting women out there. What does she think! He snaps his laptop shut.

Love, if that's what it is

The air hangs inert between the houses, the edge of the asphalt has widened into a strip of melting black quivering above the road. She is going to grill sardines on the balcony. She has made iced tea, and potato salad, and has melon chunks soaking in Muscatel. It still needs a salad, she has to buy wine, maybe a dessert, maybe strawberries.

They still haven't been seeing each other long enough to really stoke the passion. Under different circumstances, if they were twenty years old, if there were no children involved, if there weren't any lives with huge voids in them, they would be gorging themselves on each other until the fiercest hunger was stilled. And only then would it become clear what else there was; then they'd either decide to live together, or they'd end it, cheerfully or sadly, and move on to other partners—definitely in her case; as for him, don't forget he's coming from a different place: he's had one wife, and then he's had Sev, and he tends to shy away from adventure. Was Terri really the love of his life? Or was it just a matter of chance, of timing, or a need for stability?

She chooses the fish. At her next stop she buys wine, lettuce, scallions, strawberries, pomegranate, and lemons. The café terraces are crowded, people don't seem to have anything to attend to, the heat just won't let up, the nights are endless. Suddenly she remembers the barbecue, and charcoal, and the storage bin on the balcony. Does she still have a bag of briquettes? She doesn't know. She turns and goes back into the store, but they're out of charcoal. Her bin—she opens it mentally—she wishes she was more organized, people who are organized know what they have, she's bought so many sets of socket wrenches that she could start a business. In the third store she tries, she finds a disposable grill.

She undresses the way he will undress her later, and turns on the shower. David's skin is smooth and soft, he loves it when she caresses him, he lies there letting himself be fondled. Sometimes she tells him he should tell her she's sweet; then, when he says it, it never sounds as if he's obeying an order, but as if he really means it. When he says it, it makes the insides of her cheeks itch.

Her friends Lilly and Iris asked her if she would call it a relationship, the thing she has with David. Lilly took a dim view of the way he was keeping her a secret from his children, from his friends, of how he didn't want to see her anywhere but at her place and wasn't interested in meeting her son. The two of them sat down with her and expressed their doubts; they were concerned for her in a rather patronizing way. "I want you to have someone who's really *there* for you," Lilly said, and the bland platitude made Sev feel embarrassed for her. "So, as far as he's concerned the affair isn't legitimate. How can that be love?" asked Iris. But what is legitimate, then? Sev thought to herself. Whose business is it anyway—love—except of the people involved? What does it matter to Sev whether anyone else knows where David is, or that he's with her?

Standing in front of her closet, she pulls on a pair of shorts and a navy shirt with a pattern of little white birds, then takes them off again. She tries on a dress and rejects that too.

She once had the nerve to tell David she doesn't really think much of the whole nuclear family concept, that when she's picking her kid up from school, she doesn't really see anything particularly enviable about the parents who are not divorced; that the couples she sees tend to give the impression they're cramping each other's style, standing in each other's way, a stone around each other's necks. That's the only time she has ever seen him get even the slightest bit huffy about something she said. It promptly made her wonder if it wasn't an opinion from a different time in her life. All of a sudden, as if prying some new acquisition she never knew she wanted out of its plastic bubble, she felt herself longing to be part of a couple, with him, the way Lilly and Iris meant, the way he'd been a couple with his wife, a family unit, never questioned, indivisible; to be part of the same thing. It isn't something she's never wanted, it's just something she hasn't been able to achieve.

She thinks about Ernst, who once told her it wasn't that he thought they had a good relationship; it was just that he wanted to change it, together, into something better, that divorce was a pitiful form of weakness, that he was prepared to do anything to save the marriage. Prepared to do anything, she said, but useless at getting it done.

She thinks of David's hands on her body, of his mouth on hers, of his body in her arms, of his arms around her, of his soft, smooth skin, of his eyes, his thick, rough hair, the rest of him, all of it.

If she were married to him, she too would no doubt be driven up the wall by his faithful dependability. The fact that they even met is so improbable that it must mean something. That's the kind of thing she's been thinking lately, she decodes significance from the details of their lives, signs that taken together lead to some inevitable conclusion. For instance, she thinks there's a chance they each lost their virginity at the exact same moment in time. He at twenty-four, to Terri; Sev at sixteen, on the hard forest floor with sand in her butt.

She's still parked in front of the closet in her underwear. He'll be here in less than ten minutes, and she still has no idea what clothes she wants him to remove when he undresses her. And she still has to finish the dishes, and clear the table, and remove the seeds from the pomegranate. She tries on the shorts and bird shirt again. Is loneliness a condition or a personality trait? Is love something that catches you unawares or something that's fabricated? Doesn't being yourself with another person actually mean being someone you'd like to be in their eyes?

The door downstairs buzzes open and he

takes the elevator up. His shirt is plastered to his back. How often has he been here by now, twenty, twenty-five times? He needs a shower. Without ever discussing it, Terri and he had both decided he smelled. He always used to take a shower before having sex, and afterwards she always rinsed him off herself. It had surreptitiously become part of the image he had of himself. He'd never really thought about it before, he'd never been conscious of it, until Sev trained her olfactory senses on him, inhaling him not for his sake but for her own pleasure. His shame had grown endlessly, and then— pop—it had disappeared.

She's so uncomplicated, he thinks, she's so much freer than him, than anyone he knows. She's having this affair with him, sleeping with him, lovingly, but without a need for security, she isn't lonely, she isn't insecure, as he is, she is much more liberated than Terri, who only left him to be with someone else, although she pretends the two things aren't connected.

He rounds the corner and there she stands, as always, in the doorway, as she has done every time except the very first. He stops a moment and takes it all in, hears the voice inside him saying that this isn't really possible—no obligations, no promises, no till death us do part—that he's a cad. He kisses her in order to silence the voice. Arousal does the trick. He puts his hands on her bottom, feels her tits against his chest.

"Am I a party tonight?"

"Yes. Birthday party for a colleague, she's turning fifty, has spared no expense."

"So it'll be pretty late."

"That's quite possible."

"Great, so we'll have time."

"What do you need time for?"

He pads through her living room on the balls of his feet, past the piano, through the tunnel of her closet, to the bed on the wall opposite. The first time, the twentieth. He feels a surge of happiness. If Terri only knew. He isn't as dead, as dull, as sexless as she thinks. If she only knew what he's been discovering about himself, about women, now that she is no longer the measure of all things.

Sev takes her fill of him, that's what it feels like, she smells and licks, she sits on top of him without pretense or affectation, she doesn't make faces, she knows what she wants, she guides him, she fucks him, she looks at him, she growls and pants, she works herself into a swoon of delight, sometimes she'll spur him on or tell him what to do, she holds on to him tight. He thinks of dance lessons when he was a boy, how he would have much preferred to be led over having to lead; of the girls who, with their bodies close to his, their hands in his hand and his hand on their backs, waited for him to lead them with a touch of scorn, or what he took to be scorn. And he lets go completely, he lies back and surrenders, she kisses him, she rubs her body on his sweaty chest, she licks his lips, he's weeping again, she licks his eyes, he gazes at her, she may be crying too, inside him there's a hole that's slowly being filled up, it's as if she's enveloping him in love, wrapping him up, as if he's a drop of water in an ocean, a child in a nonverbal universe, bathed in the glow of the mother's unconditional love. But that's not a real thing, naturally, and there's sharks in the ocean and …

"David!" She's calling to him, she has her hand on his cheek, forces him to look at her. "Calm down, calm now, calm," she says, caressing him, he's trembling, he's crying, snot dripping from his nose.

"Stay there like that for a bit, please?"

"Aren't you getting crushed?"

"I love getting crushed by you."

She had stroked his back until he calmed down. He told her he'd been drowning; she said she'd noticed. Once he was calm, she started again, gently and ever so slowly, until she climaxed. Now he feels light and empty and maybe even happy.

"Your stomach's rumbling."

"That was your stomach."

"I've caught us some fish."

"Yum."

"Maybe we can take in a movie, later, after the fish."

"Uh, no!"

"Oh no?"

"No, I want to be with you."

"But I'd be with you at the cinema, wouldn't I?"

"No, no, no. I want to stay here, to be home, indoors, with you." Imagine if he bumped into someone, someone who knows his kids, someone who knows Terri, someone who knows someone who knows Terri or his kids.

"Come on, let's get up, let's have something to eat." She climbs off him, plants a kiss on his chest, strokes his arms; he buries his hands in her hair, pulls her head up to his face, kisses her warm cheeks.

"The first time I saw you, just the back of your head as you were lighting the candle, your dark hair cascading down your naked back, you turned around and then I saw your face."

"And now you're here."

"Now I'm here, I seem to keep coming back."

"But today ..."

"Today it's the last time, it's the last time today, that's why no movies; the last time, this very last time I want to stay home with you, to be close to you."

He chews on a piece of bread, he squeezes lemon over the fish, it's delicious, what she cooks is always delicious. She's resting her feet in his lap.

"Maybe I should tell them. Maybe it's time to tell them at home."

"Yes."

"Hmm ..."

"Why not?"

"I don't dare, it's too soon, it's too ..."

"Scary? How do you think they'll ..."

"Angry? Terrified?"

"Terrified?"

"That I too will ..."

"Leave them?"

"Yes."

"But you're not going to, are you?"

"No."

"But?"

"They won't trust it."

"Time will tell."

"I don't know, I don't think I'm ready. Is that bad?"

"No, no, it's fine this way, isn't it?"

"I think it's very fine this way. You are very fine, this way."

"What way? Like this? How?" They laugh. He strokes her calves.

"Krista's still not talking to Terri. Terri thinks it's my fault, she thinks I'm shutting her out, she thinks I'm setting the children against her, feeding them anger. I tell her they don't need me for that. It's not true, in any case. I'm the one pushing for contact. But Kris is fifteen, you can't make a girl of fifteen do anything she doesn't want to do, what's the point of forcing her to talk to her mother? If she were six, then okay, fine. Today I had a message from the family therapist: we can see her next week. We'll go just the two of us, and then later with the girls. You'd think Terri would be thrilled, but she's just pissed off because I made the appointment for a time when she had something else going on, and now she has to change it." It all comes pouring out, his heart, all the agonizing about whether he's doing the right thing, and she listens and she pours him another glass of wine and soon, perhaps, she will lead him back to her bed, to crush him flat, with her body, with her love, but why, for God's sake, does he really deserve it?

She calls a cab for him and watches him get in downstairs and be driven off. She empties the rest of the bottle into her glass. She wanted him to spend the night, is there any way to be closer to someone than when he's asleep, when he's sleeping in your arms? She thinks of the river running between her and Felix, between her and Ernst, between her and the world, and now it's between her and David. She remembers the joke about the two dumb blondes on opposite sides of a river. One puts her hands to her mouth and yells, How do I get *ooover* to the other side? The other one also puts her hands to her mouth and bellows back, You're *aaaaalready* there! She thinks about David's world, the nightmare that is matrimony; about her own life. As long as he makes love to me the way he does, she thinks, so gently and fully, it's balm for the pain as well as pain with the balm. That's the funny thing about love: love is the medicine you wouldn't need if the love didn't exist.

FALL

What are you doing here?

He is here, in her house. He's sitting at the kitchen table. He doesn't need her to bring him any dry clothes. She's been upstairs to change into dry jeans and a dry T-shirt herself, and she's brought him a towel.

"You're melting." She points at the floor under his chair, where a puddle has slowly been forming. He grins. He's wearing a rather dressy shirt underneath a shiny Adidas bomber jacket, black pants, no djellaba. They were caught in the rainstorm, they were sitting on their bench when it suddenly grew dark and the rain started pouring down on their heads as if they were being doused with buckets of water. They'd screamed and laughed and he'd shouted, more animated than she'd ever seen him, The sky is falling! And then she remembered David was at work and Ally was supposed to go straight to Terri's after school to do her homework.

"Do you want anything to drink? Coke, tea?"

"Coke, I guess." There's what remains of a plum cake on the counter under a mesh fly cover. She cuts a couple of slices and puts them on a plate.

"How long has it been since your dad died?"

"Four years."

She hands him a Coke. She now also knows he's seventeen, and he's in twelfth grade at a school across town. She knows that he has to babysit for his little brother and sister two afternoons a week when his mother is at her job. That his older brother works in a hotel and lives in a rented flat and almost never comes home. He nibbles at the plum cake and there's still water dripping off him onto the floor.

"He drowned at sea, in Morocco. We almost stayed. Mimoun was still a baby, my mom wanted to stay with her family. But after three months we came home anyway."

"I'm glad."

"Yeah."

"And, uh, do you miss him?"

"I suppose."

They eat cake, they sip Coke, when their eyes meet she smiles and he looks serious. And then they talk about school and about music, and about Morocco and about their families. He does smile when he mentions his little brother and sister, the whole time in fact, and as if he isn't aware of it. Outside it's still raining cats and dogs. When the conversation falters, which it does from time to time, she can feel how hot her cheeks are, can feel her heart pounding in her chest. She looks at his downy moustache and sees the golden specks in his brown eyes. And suddenly she thinks, I'm definitely not kissing him, what a dumb idea—thinking about kissing a boy is tied to having to tell Tirza about it, to impress her or keep up with her. But now that that motive is gone—if she made out with Rafik, there's no way she'd tell anyone, because she won't let anything or anybody spoil it, especially not Tirza, who'll call him *that Moroccer*—she realizes there's no need for kissing. She just wants to *be* with him, be close to him, it doesn't matter what he does, even if he doesn't say anything and just looks at her, or doesn't. Just as she's starting to wonder what's next, if they should go do something, if she should show him her room or if that's too embarrassing, or if, following that train of thought, it makes a difference that he's Muslim, and if he's actually a devout Muslim, or if the djellaba means he is—or maybe they could go downstairs and watch something on Netflix, and what would they watch?—the door opens and Ally barges into the kitchen, dripping wet.

"Jesus."

All three gape at each other. Ally looks down at the puddle at her feet.

"I'm melting!"

Krista feels the blood rush to her cheeks. She doesn't dare look at Rafik.

"This is my little sister, Ally."

"Hey. I'm Rafik."

"Hey." Why is Krista acting so weird and why is she so red in the face? Ally wonders. All the way home in the pouring rain, she was hoping she'd find Krista home so she could tell her that Terri wasn't there but that that guy, the joker who stole their mother, as David had suddenly called him the last time he tried to explain it to her again, had walked out of Terri's bedroom. In his underwear. What he'd said to her.

Her phone is vibrating in her pocket non-stop. Terri of course. Well, she isn't going to answer it. She doesn't give a hoot about that man being at her mother's apartment, but she does mind that her mother broke her promise *again*, that she forgot Ally was coming and that that man, that Lucas, turns out to be such a creep, that too.

"Do you want some of Dad's plum cake?"

"Sure." She sits down at the table.

"Aren't you going to change your clothes first?"

"Oh, right."

She goes upstairs and strips off her wet clothes, leaving them trailing on the bathroom floor. Who is that boy, anyway? She's never seen him before. Does Krista have a boyfriend now, or what?

She'd walked into her mom's apartment to find the windows all fogged up, and, from the sound of it, Terri in the shower. She'd taken out her homework and spread it on the table: German, Dutch grammar, math. It was a compromise: twice a week Terri would come home from work early and help Ally with her homework, which David wasn't supervising well enough, according to Terri, though as far Ally is concerned there's no need for him to, since she always does her homework anyway; and stay for dinner, often yucky food, not only gross and much too plain, but often raw or burnt too—Terri doesn't seem to know how to cook anymore, it's as if in divvying up their possessions, they've reassigned the domestic skills as well. Terri asks her questions at dinner, but never seems to remember the answers; every week she asks her to bring Isabel next time. Today Ally was going to tell her she wants to go to tennis camp in the fall break. If Terri said it was ridiculously expensive, she would tell her she'd pay for some of it herself. She's saved at least €200 and she's prepared to spend all of it. She had put the kettle on for tea, then the bathroom door opened behind her, she turned and there he stood, a man, in a pair of checked boxers, with wet hair, rubbing some oily stuff into his chest with his hands. Ally nearly jumped out of her skin, she just stood there mutely, rooted to the spot, her back to the sink, probably with her mouth open.

"Well," he said.

She didn't say a word. He took a few steps in her direction.

"Why didn't you ring the bell? You nearly gave me a heart attack."

"But I live here."

"Well, according to what I've heard, you don't *want* to live here." What she should have said then, of course, is that according to what *she*'s heard, he doesn't live there either and is never even supposed to go there, but she kept her mouth shut, paralyzed. Which he noticed.

"I'm Lucas. Cat got your tongue?" They stood there facing each other, he in those boxer shorts and she up against the sink;

behind her the kettle was starting to steam. "The water's boiling." And when she still didn't say anything, "I'll just go get dressed."

"Where's Mommy?" She said Mommy, what an idiot! Why hadn't she said Terri, why did she have to call her Mommy to this man's face?

"No idea, Ally, she isn't here, anyway." Then he turned and walked away, into the bedroom, and shut the door. Ally turned off the kettle, packed up her schoolbag and went out into the pouring rain.

She puts on her pajamas and goes down to the kitchen. Monopoly is spread out on the table.

"Wanna play?" It's been ages since Krista has wanted to play any kind of game with her.

Upstairs, in the pocket of her discarded jeans, her phone rings for the seventh time, then goes to voicemail.

"Ally, it's Terri, sorry sorry sorry, please call me back, I was held up at work, I didn't know Lucas would still be there. You must have had a shock, but, well, now you've met him, anyway, it had to happen sometime.

Please call me back. Don't do this."

Terri hangs up, swears, picks up her bag and walks out of her office.

"Problem with one of my kids, I've got to go home," she tells her colleague. On her bike she tries calling Lucas again but he doesn't pick up either. How terribly stupid, she'd forgotten about Ally, and how could she have known that Lucas, whom she'd left behind in her bedroom at eight thirty this morning, would still be there at this hour, 2 p.m., what was he *thinking*? He's texted her: *Met Ally, you might have told me she was coming over.* She takes the familiar route to her old house. David has told her that, out of respect for Krista, she is never to arrive there unannounced, but he's got some nerve, what does he mean out of respect, officially that house still half belongs to her, fucking hell, they're her fucking children, she's allowed to go see her own fucking children, isn't she? She doesn't have the key on her, so she'll have to ring the bell. Not out of fucking respect; out of need. It has stopped raining. Her tire is flat.

For the first time in maybe a year, Ally's happy, happy the way she used to be happy, happy the way a little kid is happy, no regrets and no worries. She buys a hotel, she gets out of jail, she munches on cake and paprika potato chips. Krista is back to being good old Krista again, whose orbit she's been in her whole life, and Rafik is nice and said he likes her pajamas, even though they're really a bit too small, and dingy from too many washings, and anyway, telling someone you like their pajamas is kind of weird.

"Why aren't you at Terri's, anyway?"

"She wasn't home."

"Tssk." Krista shakes her head and tosses the dice. "Our mother," she says to Rafik, "who's given up on being our mother." And then, after a quick glance at Ally, "Our mother the whore."

Ally stiffens and feels all her defenses spring into action, always on standby to defend everyone from everyone else, but then she relaxes and smile and nods, and there's something liberating about repeating that phrase, our mother the whore.

Rafik is looking very serious.

"I wouldn't say it," says Krista, very serious too, "if I hadn't read a great long smutty sext-thread on her phone. Made me want to vomit."

Ally is gaping at her. Maybe she shouldn't have told them? Rafik is staring at her too. Maybe he's thinking her mother's behavior could rub off on her? Krista suddenly feels queasy, she shouldn't have told, naturally, it just slipped out, and suddenly, to her consternation, she starts to cry, she can't help it, and the whole story about the switched phones comes pouring out.

"Maybe she's having a midlife crisis. It may pass," says Rafik. "The parents of one of my friends are having one too, they got divorced and are both dating other people like crazy. My friend is mortified."

"Are they Muslim?"

"No, no, we don't do that sort of thing. Uh, I mean, Muslims don't do that."

"Why not?"

"We're not allowed."

"Oh."

"We have other things though."

"Oh. Yeah. You're still dripping on the floor, by the way."

"Oh."

Krista blows her nose. She opens the fridge and gives everyone another Coke.

"But what do you do about a mother like that, Rafik, what would you do?"

"You should probably let her be for a while."

"Right, that's what I'm doing."

"Yeah, that's what she's been doing, she refuses to talk to her. She's even blocked her number. And when Mom phones from the office, she hangs up on her. And she doesn't pick up if it's an unknown number. And Daddy says she can't just barge in here anymore for no reason."

"But it's driving her nuts. So she's been sending me letters."

"Letters? How many letters has she sent you, then?" asks Ally.

"Two. I did read the first, it said she didn't want to be my mother anymore." Shoot, now she's crying again! She rubs away her tears and takes a sip of Coke. "And in the second ... I don't know ... she's trying to ... I don't know ... to be my friend, or something. I don't know, I didn't finish it. It's too awful."

The doorbell rings.

"Rafik, could you please go open the door? And if it's Terri, tell her to get lost." She grabs his hands.

"How do I know if it's Terri?"

"If it's a kind of skinny lady with a scowl on her face, it's Terri," says Krista, fishing her phone out of her pocket.

"And a green coat," cries Ally.

"I'm calling David."

"Hi." He plants his hands right and left, spanning the doorway.

"Hello. This is my house. Who are you?"

"Rafik el-Omri, how do you do?" He extends a hand.

"What are you in relation to which one of mine?"

"Excuse me?"

"What are you doing here?"

"Playing Monopoly with Krista and Ally." She won't shake his hand, so he puts it back against the doorframe.

"How old are you?"

"Seventeen."

"Does David know you're here? Does David know you?"

"We haven't met yet."

"Will you please step aside so that I can come in?"

"I believe your daughters don't want you to come in."

"Ally does."

"Ally doesn't either."

"What was your name again?"

"Rafik."

"I've never heard of you."

"I'd never heard about you until today either."

"What did you hear?"

"They told me a bit about your uh, departure, about your letters to Krista, and about the WhatsApp chat with your friend."

"My what?"

"The conversation with your boyfriend, and, uh, the nature of it."

"What?" The blood drains from her cheeks. "What are you talking about?"

"She wasn't supposed to read it, of course, you didn't mean for her to read it, but it happened."

"Oh God."

"The frankness of your letters didn't help."

"Oh God, oh God."

"She didn't really read them, not the second one anyway, as she was obviously meant to do, as you meant her to, but it didn't happen, she never finished reading the second letter."

"Let me go in."

"Bad idea."

"I'll be the judge of that."

"Think of it as a handful of sand, the more firmly you squeeze to hold on to it, the faster it slips out of your grasp."

Terri stares at him. What kind of jackass is this? What's he doing lurking in her doorway lecturing her like some freaking wise guy?

"Ally! Krista! Helloooo!"

Right on cue, as if some higher force has decided to get involved, it starts to pour again. Terri stands facing the boy, that Rafik, who is barring her from entering her own house, as the rain falls on her head with pitiless indifference and streams down her face.

"You'd better go." He shuts the door in her face, and she finds herself pounding her fists on the dark-green paint.

"Open up, dammit!"

She sinks to her knees in front of the door. So it was Krista, not David. She tries to remember if the chat had anything unkind about Krista in it, but she doesn't think so. She does know, however, that the juxtaposition of sex and parents is a horror, and she would never think of confronting her daughters with it, but it was *her* phone. It's Krista's own damn fault, punishment for snooping and reading private stuff on her mother's phone. Nothing's sacred, nothing's private within a family, it only goes to show that's true. Invasion of privacy—of all the things she's endured living in this house, this last one takes the cake. She's crying now, furious, impotent; she has right on her side, but being right is no use to her now.

"Terri? Jesus."

"Hello to you too."

David is leaning on his bicycle, one foot on the ground. In head-to-toe rain gear, an amorphous plastic apparition, she thinks: my spouse.

"I'm not allowed inside."

"So why don't you just run on home."

"Did you just tell me to run on home?"

"Yes, that's what I said."

"You've turned the children against me."

"Not at all. Let's discuss this tomorrow at Pauline's, shall we?"

"Oh yeah, Pauline." She gives a deep, hopeless sigh, "the marriage counselor."

"Family therapist."

"There's a boy in there, Rafik's his name, Krista's boyfriend, I think, at least three years older than her."

"Boyfriend? Well, I doubt that. Come on, Terri, get up, go home."

"No."

David gets off his bike, parks it on the stand, turns her bike, which she'd left leaning against the wall, pointing in the right direction.

"My tire is flat." He looks. Her tire isn't just flat, her wheel is also badly dented.

"Did you ride here on that?"

"Yes."

"Idiot. Wait here. I'll go see what's going on inside and then I'll take you home."

"I'm coming in with you."

"No." He brushes past her, opens the door and immediately shuts it again.

She gets to her feet; turning her head, she finds herself eye to eye with the next-door neighbor at her kitchen window, just inches from their front door. She gives her the finger and starts walking.

When half an hour later she's reached her own door, drenched to the skin, she realizes she's left her keys in her bicycle lock. She takes out her phone but it's dead. Out of batteries, or it got soaked. She's not going to sit shivering outside another locked door like some sorry bundle of misery; she makes herself walk on. Not back across the bridge, and not to Lucas's, but to find a charger somewhere and call a locksmith. To be independent. The humiliation of that Moroccan kid telling her about her chat with Lucas *and the nature of it*. And finding out that Kris hasn't read her letters. And *why don't you just run on home?* David in his ugly rain suit, she'd rather get wet. She walks into a café, borrows a charger, orders a cup of tea and sits down in a corner with her back against the radiator.

"Are you okay?" The girl brings over the box of teabags and hands her a tea towel. She must be a sight. She forces her teeth to stop chattering, she nods and smiles: "I'm fine, really, lost my keys." Lost everything. She dries her hair and her hands. Her jacket is more or less waterproof, so the top half of her body is reasonably dry. If that Pauline woman tomorrow won't support her in wanting to be in touch with Krista, forcing the girl to see her if necessary, and instead goes along with David's namby-pamby give-her-time approach, she'll grab the woman by whatever she's wearing and drag her across the desk.

Parent-teacher conference

They have to wait in the corridor. Sev ambles past the drawings hanging on the walls, the children's self-portraits ringed with things that define them, or just the things they like best. Hendrik's head is wreathed in Legos, an iPad, a soccer ball, a rainbow of colored pencils. Ernst, perched on a desk, appears to be in middling bad shape, could be worse. The parents of what's-his-name walk out of the classroom and the teacher waves them inside. They sit down across from her.

"So! Hendrik!" She gathers some papers.

"How do *you* think it's going?" They both think it's going pretty well, and the teacher confirms it, she shows them results, spreading them out on the desk. Ernst runs his finger along the lines, like a child just learning to read. His finger stops at a slight dip in the proficiency level. "Uh, yes, that's, let me see, I think it was a momentary lapse, he did the same work later and it was fine." With Ernst sitting so close, Sev can smell him. "He does seem a bit tired these days. Have you noticed? He fell asleep in class the other day."

Ernst and Sev look at each other. He's probably thinking she isn't being a very good parent, he's probably thinking that she must be thinking *he* isn't being a very good parent. She resists asking what day that was, whose week it was when it happened.

"He isn't a very good sleeper," Ernst says.

"Well, when he was younger, maybe, but he's a pretty good sleeper nowadays, don't you think?"

The teacher is probably thinking: divorced parents, only child, poor kid. Nothing else out of the ordinary, the two of them will discuss the sleepiness issue, the teacher will let them know if it happens again. Which one? It makes no difference, they're religious about keeping each other informed. That's wonderful. It's not always so harmonious. All three nod cheerfully. If Ernst hadn't spent the rest of the time jabbering about his own school days, they'd have been out of there long before the scheduled ten minutes. She has no intention of bringing it up with him, however, since setting the intensity of her irritation against the duration of the offense, she knows mentioning it would waste even more time, and wouldn't make her any less annoyed. Just try not to let it bother you too much.

"That went well didn't it? So, everything's fine." He lights up a cigarette.

"Yes."

"So, really, he's doing great. Just great." Yes, she thinks, say it one more time. "Just great."

"Yes."

"Feel like going for a drink?"

"Where is Hendrik?"

"At the neighbors'."

"No, I think I'll just head on home. I still

have … things to do. Another time, all right?"

"I do want to go over a few things again soon, though," he says.

"What sort of things do you want to go over?"

"Just things, all sorts of stuff."

When they were still living together, she often felt as if he were sitting on top of her, squeezing all the air out of her.

"Okay, you say when," she says finally.

"Okay, I'll try to find a time."

"I'll see you Sunday in any case, when you bring Hendrik home, won't I?"

"Bring him to your apartment."

"Yes, that's what I meant."

"My place is his home too."

"Yeah, yeah, sorry. Give him my love, will you?"

"But don't we have to discuss his sleepiness?"

"Yes, I take it we do." She turns her feet back towards him again. "I don't know, Ernst, if it happened once, maybe it's not that concerning? Was it just coincidence? When he's with me he doesn't go to bed late, eight thirty or so, and then he'll still read a bit in bed."

"Same at my place. Well ... okay then. We'll just have to keep an eye on it."

"Right."

"But does he strike you as being tired?"

"Well, uh, no."

"Maybe we're not watching him closely enough."

"He dozes off at school one time, and his report card is all As. Let's not make a mountain out of a molehill."

"But it would be a shame if we ..."

"Missed something. Yes, I get it." She hates the way he's always trying to stall, slowing things down; sandbags on her tail is what it feels like, what it used to feel like, what it felt like most of the time they were together. When it was over, she couldn't feel much relief; for months she was sick with guilt. During those first six months he kept calling to demand an explanation. Why had she broken up with him, always the same question, and then all her different variations on the answer. The next six months he was no longer asking why she'd ended it; now he wanted to know why she'd ever started it in the first place. After a year, he stopped asking those questions.

"How are you otherwise?"

"Me?"

"Yes."

"Well, pretty good, I'd say."

"What are you up to?"

"I've got a few gigs here and there."

"Okay."

"And how are you doing?"

"A little better." It's always a little better.

"That's good."

"Yeah."

"I have to go."

"I understand."

David is coming over in an hour. Early this morning she prepared veal scallops, and there is endive. But she wants to go out with him instead, to a restaurant, to get off their island.

A silly waste of time

She changes into her running clothes, ties
her hair in a ponytail, rubs her knees. If
you're going out running anyway, Lucas
said, you could stop at my place and drop off
the key to your new place. But the little pocket
on her sleeve holds only one key, her own.
She shuts her door and weaves her way down
the cluttered front stairs. She runs to the end
of her street, the street she also used to live
on when she was a student, when the thought
of running never occurred to her, except to
catch a tram, and when she could never have

imagined that her life would follow such a conventional route: married, two children, housing development, the suburbs, steady job. What form did she imagine it would take back then, what did she dream of? And suddenly she's convinced that's what the problem was: her dreams were ill-defined, there may have been a general sense of purpose or adventure, of a future life and loves, but nothing concrete; and besides, it all lay well ahead, it would come eventually, of its own accord, as does summer, or the next century, or as morning follows night. There was another boy, Richard, she knows David thinks she slept with him, she encouraged him to think so, she wanted to be taken for a woman of the world; why did she want to pretend to be, but not be one? Why was she such a bloody prude? "Can you tell us why you're so angry?" Pauline asked half an hour into the session. Whereas for the entire first half hour she had been the reasonable one there in that frigging office with the woodsy wallpaper, the one who knew what she was about, the one who knew what she wanted: a new chapter in her life, in which things were moving forward, in which David did have a marginal role, but her children naturally belonged with her. David had been the unreasonable one, full of complaints both big and small, full of self-pity; the therapist, quite unfairly, had taken his side. "I am on nobody's side," she'd replied when Terri said it, "my only concern is for the wellbeing of your children; if I'm on anyone's side, I'm on theirs." As if she would know what's best for children she's never even met! As if David and Ally and Krista and Terri herself were just cast in specific roles, and are now expected to follow some fucking script. A Lucas-thought, that. Or her own? She jogs across a square and jumps from one foot to the other until the light turns green and she can cross. She can feel her legs, the lactic acid draining from her calves, the running is making her stiff, she should be doing yoga as well. She takes a deep breath, it's nice weather out, not as hot as before, the days are getting shorter, her heart is pumping and she's starting to sweat. Pauline decided she was at fault, how can she trust the woman now and allow her to have a role in her life? David accused her of breaking her promise to Ally not to let Lucas into her home. She said she was willing to discuss that with Ally, but not with them. She refused to talk about Lucas at all. She told them that as a consequence of her decision to leave, some things are private now, her love life, for one. David rolled his eyes and threw up his hands, openly venting his disgust. She's come to the growing realization that David doesn't really love her, even if he claims that's where it hurts. Their marriage was just an arrangement; his behavior now proves it. He doesn't even like her, a fact that all these years he's been covering up with the charade that a marriage like theirs really is. Wanting to be with her, to be together, was an idea, an idée fixe, and now it's off the table. She stared at the green mist stippled between the gray-brown tree trunks on the wall, she wished she could disappear into it, away from this phony therapy freak show.

She runs into the park, which is already taking on the colors of fall. She hits her stride, her sweat and her breath push out her anger, and her mind starts making room for other thoughts. She thinks about Lucas, and how she's torn between lust and a growing dislike. Maybe this thing is a way of compensating for her past prudishness, a juvenile attempt at making up for lost time. He isn't even nice. Lucas calls love a silly waste of time. She sometimes thinks he's a psychopath, without the bloodthirstiness, but also without empathy or interest in anything but himself. She's not going to give him her key, she's going to end it. And then she'll start playing nice, with Pauline and her wallpaper, and she'll give Krista some space, all the space she needs, even, and she'll tell Ally she's sorry, without drama, without getting into intimate details, and she'll go along with the parenting plan, and with the financial arrangement, she'll accept the consequences of that financial arrangement, she's even looking forward to the frugality she'll have to impose on herself, no new clothes, no purchases, no vacations: austerity. She'll sign the divorce papers. She'll put herself on a diet of books and films to feed her soul and fulfill her needs. She'll set herself free, truly free.

As she's leaving the park, she spots Simone. Before she has a chance to turn and pretend she didn't, Simone has spotted her too. They haven't spoken since that awful evening, she knows David speaks to Hugo often, probably to complain about her.

"Hi."

"Terri, good to see you, how are you?"

"Yeah."

"How's it going?"

"Well. I live here now, over there, on ..." Her arm hovers in the air.

"I know, I heard." Stress on *know*, emphasis on *heard*.

"Yeah, yeah, you hear everything, of course."

"The basic facts, anyway, but how *are* you, how are you doing?" Emphasis on *are*, to express concern. People who want to have a conversation with you when you're out running, putting you off your stride, making the sweat chill down your body. "Are you and Krista speaking again?"

"Oh, sure." Who says you have to tell the truth, in this kind of encounter? It's not as if the rubbernecker opposite her is being very truthful herself. "Yes, fortunately, it's all back to normal." And before Simone, with her raised eyebrows, can get her claws in any deeper: "And how is Jane doing?"

Simone says everything's fine and some other generalities, fluffing her hair with her hands, a weird gesture, taken out of context. Terri starts to stretch the muscles in one thigh, then the other. Then she twists her hips from side to side.

"You know what it is," Terri finally says, "it's not that I'm happy now, it's a lot less simple than I thought, than everyone thinks, it's just that I'm seeing my unhappiness with very different eyes."

"Oh."

"And realizing stuff."

"Stuff."

"Yes. About marriages."

"Oh."

"About losing yourself. About making the other person feel smaller."

"Yes, yes. But ..."

"Standing still when you're in the middle of a run isn't good for you, you know."

"No."

"So. Bye!"

She sprints off.

Terri is standing in the door opening in her purple Lycra jogging suit. He hasn't seen or spoken to her since the unfortunate encounter with her daughter. He finds it irritating that she's the one who decides when they meet. Maybe he should stop seeing her, too many issues, too much grief these days. But wanting to end it makes it seem as if it's an actual relationship. They fuck. That's it. On a regular basis. He mustn't let himself get distracted. Not by her emotions, not by his own emotions. He's got far better things to do in the world.

Terri walks past him into the kitchen and guzzles two glasses of water at the sink. He walks up behind her, he can smell her fresh sweat.

"It's been a year," she says.

"What?" He puts his hands on her hips.

"It's been just about a year, I think, since we first …"

He presses his erection against her butt. She isn't going to want to mark that milestone, surely, with champagne and sentimental shit? She leans into him, he puts his hands on her tits, on top of the tight wet shirt. He hates it when something needs to be evaluated, he hates it when intelligent people use their intelligence to bite their own tails, so to speak, when they start dissecting their feelings under the microscope like rare specimens. He starts to pull down her pants. She automatically responds by thrusting out her bottom, and once the pants are down at her feet she picks up one foot and spreads her legs apart. Lucas starts fingering her, and she rests her forearms on the cool counter. She should be alone, she thinks, there's no such thing as a waste of time, and even if there was, it would be impossible to get it back. She should only have sex with Lucas if it no longer matters to her, but if it doesn't matter to her, then there's no reason to do it anymore.

"Lucas?"
  "Terri?"
  "Stop it, will you."
  "What?"

She turns around. She looks at him. She smiles.

"I'm going. I ... I'm done. I'm leaving."

On the other side of the river, Krista slips her hand into Rafik's hand. The sun hangs low over the highway, bathing the bushes on the acoustic wall in a fiery orange light. Ally is in her bedroom, she's lined up all her stuffed animals along one wall, she's perfectly aware that she's getting to be too old for them, but she doesn't care, nobody needs to know.

David rings Sev's doorbell but instead of pushing the buzzer, she takes the elevator down. Outside the building's front door, she puts a hand on David's cheek. He looks at her, shocked to see her for the first time in broad daylight, instead of the filtered light coming in through a window. "Come," she says, and leads him away. Ernst is boiling water for tea, and Hendrik, in Ernst's kitchen, is making a drawing for Sev, of a gigantic ship; he misses her and he tried calling her but she didn't pick up.

The end

"I was at this book launch, someone I've known for about fifteen years and who's grown more and more ascetic over time. At first he was fat and fun and he used to drink a lot, but now he has the body of a marathon runner and he lives like a monk, in Italy somewhere, in some ghost town. His wife does something important, I always forget what exactly, she flies all over the world while he stays home alone, in silence. Strangely enough the change in him doesn't seem to be reflected in his books, which are still about the problems of urbanites of his generation. His stories did always have a mystical side to them, even when he was still living here in the city and often hung out with us at the café. Anyway, his sixth book came out, it was great, he gave a good talk, his publisher too, and afterwards we went to the café and sat around for hours shooting the breeze."

"Who's we?"

"Oscar himself, his wife, his publisher, a few friends of his, I know them all too, my friend Anne, a kid I'd never seen before, I don't think he's one of us but for some reason was swept along from the bookstore to the café. I must have announced, 'Okay then, just one for the road' at least four times before I actually drank my last glass and walked out to my bike. It was only eleven, still a decent time to get home, only I hadn't eaten anything except for a few cheese crackers."

"Were you drunk?"

"Tipsy."

"Nice."

Sev looks at David sitting across from her. Nice, he says, with a rakish kind of look, like a schoolboy, she thinks, like a schoolboy who thinks a tipsy woman is exciting because of the implied lack of inhibition.

"On the way home I stopped at a snack bar for a shawarma sandwich. There were two other people in there, a guy of about thirty, barefoot, sitting at his laptop eating French fries, and a short Moroccan kid with a frizzy ponytail poking out under his hat. At some point, the kid, his name was Ali ..."

"Did you know him?"

"No. Ali calls out to the guy with the bare feet: Hey man, what are you studying? The other one turns his head and says: Nothing, man, I'm no longer a student. What do you do, then? asks Ali. Pro athlete, the guy says, pro athlete and creative brainstormer. For some reason Ali and I both start to laugh. What kind of pro, Ali wants to know, and the guy says he's a kitesurfer. They talk for a while about IJmuiden and about the wind and about Velsen, where the guy lives and where Ali once got himself beaten up. Racist motives, Ali clarifies. And what kind of work do you do, he asks again. Creative brainstorming for small and medium-sized companies. Ali shakes his head, looks at me, points at the kitesurfer with open palms as if he's about to introduce us, and says, It's impossible to tell just from looking at someone what he does, isn't it? I say that's true. And what is it with the bare feet, man? Ali then asks, and you should introduce yourself. His questions and the way he asks them are very direct, but also quite sweet somehow, because he's genuinely interested, I think to myself. The guy says he stayed in bed for a year. What? cries Ali and looks at me again. A year? Hey, man, what do you mean, do you mean that literally, do you mean you literally stayed in bed for a year, or do you mean something else? But the guy means it literally, he was injured, and mentally he wasn't doing that well either. Boy oh boy, says Ali and now the guy starts to pack up his computer and put on his shoes, so he did have them with him after all. Creative brainstorming, Ali mutters again under his breath, and takes a sip of his soda. What do *you* do, then? I now ask, and Ali says he's a night porter at a fancy hotel in the city center. He entertains us with a few anecdotes about adulterers, drug dealers, a suicide, and I picture him in his uniform, how small he must look without his hat or his baggy clothes. I ask him what he thinks I do. Ali looks at me, sizing me up, cocks his head left, then right, narrows his eyes, moves his torso back and forth a couple of times and then asks, his voice rising: Teacher? No, man, says the kitesurfer, who now has his coat on, swinging his bag over his shoulder: Writer. I'd been under the impression he'd never even glanced my way. He's right, I say. Ali claps his hands. How did you know that, he wants to know. Age, coat, time of day, equipment, says the kitesurfer, pointing at my bag. It's true that my bag is full of books, but you can't see that from the outside."

"Jesus."

"The guy left and Ali and I went on talking about books a bit. Ali likes it best if it's all really happened, and he advised me to write that way from now on. If it's really happened, you know, he said, then you *feel* it. He told me about his favorite book, it was about a failed assassination attempt on Hassan II, the king of Morocco, and one about someone who was held captive underground for many years. It was a fantastic book, he'd read it three, four times in a row. I asked him how he'd come to choose that particular book. You're smart, Ali said, although I hadn't really meant anything with my question. I spent a year in prison, he said, and in the clink there's two things you can do: you can hang around smoking pot or you can read a book. We both nodded thoughtfully, as if I'd faced the same choice. He went on to tell me that he thought the kitesurfer had probably been in prison too, that his crowd called it 'a year in bed.' He also said it was a stroke of luck he'd been locked up for a violent crime, because the hotel did screen its employees, but only for theft. They'd never have offered him the job otherwise. I said night porter was the perfect job for getting a lot of reading done, but he shook his head. Not a chance, he said, perfect my ass, I want a girlfriend, and a kid and everything, that's not going to happen when you work nights. We shook hands, he said, Just call me Ali, as if he really went by a different name, and I introduced myself to him too."

"And then?"

"I went home."

"Hey, uh …"

"Yes?"

"You're not writing about us, are you?"

"No, not really, I write fiction, not memoir."

David isn't exactly at ease. As Sev was telling her story he kept shifting almost imperceptibly in his chair. His eyes flitted about, he wasn't giving her the steady, grave gaze she's used to.

Dishes are set in front of them, tuna tartare, shrimp croquettes. She offers him a piece of buttered bread.

"All right, tell me, what's been going on with you?"

"Therapy. Family therapy. Just Terri and me. And Pauline, the therapist, who's okay, really very okay, actually, very nice, very experienced, sixty or so, for her it's about the children, the children are the important thing."

They're quiet. They forget to raise their glasses.

"And then? What else did you do?"

"I don't know, I baked an apple pie."

"Bring me a piece next time."

"Yes! Of course I will." He looks troubled, as if it was a reproach.

"Just to taste."

"Yes, yes, of course, apple pie? Or something else, I do a great raspberry tart."

"Hey."

"Yes?"

"You could just say: This is Sev, couldn't you, you don't have to say I'm your girlfriend, do you?"

"What?" Is she reading his thoughts?

"If you bumped into someone you know."

"Sure."

"Because I'm not really your girlfriend, am I?"

"No."

"Or if it's a friend, Hugo for instance, why can't you just tell him the real story? You could say: This is Sev, and then later on tell him what's going on, what this is."

"Why would I tell him?"

"So that you can talk about it. So that you can understand it, so that you'll give yourself permission to lead a larger life, more than just being the spurned husband taking care of his daughters, because it *is* larger, because there's someone inside you who isn't a father or a husband or an ex-husband, but David, a grown-up, a tender lover." At the word "lover," he glances at the tables to their right and left again. She can't help laughing.

"What are you laughing about?"

"It's your life, David, why should you be ashamed?"

The plates are cleared, they order a glass of red each and a bottle of water. Mineral, she says, Still, he says; he defers. Next to them a new group sits down, Spaniards, from the sound of it.

"They won't eavesdrop on us, anyway," she whispers.

"For you it's different."

"What do you think it's like for me?"

"I don't know. You're so free, so self-sufficient." She looks at him, and doesn't move. Here it comes. "You don't need anyone. You eat shawarma and hang out with Moroccan delinquents." Is this irony? she asks herself; she doesn't think so. "I have no idea what motivates you, why you want a lover instead of a relationship, no strings attached, why do you want that, why with me, what for?"

The waiter brings the wine and the water, neither of them speaks, There it is, she thinks, the river, or perhaps it isn't a river running between herself and someone else, but a moat encircling her.

"I had to go to a parent-teacher conference at school, with Ernst. So there I was sitting next to him. I have trouble fitting our years together into the story of my life. I could tell you that I wanted to have a baby, that I had a hankering for domesticity, for security, who knows, maybe it made me feel safe, the fact that it was all so calm and easy when it began. I wasn't really in love, I think, maybe you need the love as a lubricant for later, even if it's nothing but a memory by then. Also, maybe he was a different man when I met him than the man he eventually turned into. Maybe I *was* in love, maybe the man he later turned into came to block out the man I first met; I do have a vague notion of a certain spark, an original take on things, an aesthetic view of the world, not modern, a bit eccentric perhaps, memories of having a good time with him, museums, hikes, reading to each other, *Don Quixote* in its entirety, for one. He grew depressed, and I never knew depression could ravage a man's personality so terribly, you think it's him just being himself, only in a moodier key, but that's not what it is, it eats you up inside until there's just about nothing left of you. I tried to step into the breach, I performed all the daily tasks necessary for his existence that other people didn't see. I worked up his notes if that was something he needed for his work, I took the tests for his refresher courses, I drove him to his work or to his appointments. I tried to keep him afloat, I was his external radar, helping him put things into perspective. He would tell me the same stories over and over again, the same old story of his life, he'd start at the beginning and proceed to recite a string of traumatic and humiliating things that had happened to him. So I began telling the story of his life back to him, only I gave him an alternate version, starting from the beginning and turning it into a string of triumphs that showed how creative and resilient he was; I tried to blunt the things he was so angry about by pointing out how hurt he was. I poured all my energy and improvisational skills into supporting him; I'd never before worn myself out so thoroughly in catering to another person's needs, but it did feel as if there was light at the end of the tunnel, that it might succeed, that with a superhuman effort, at some point the boulder would get to the top of the mountain, crest the summit, and roll down into the verdant valley below, and then we'd be home free. In the meantime I tried to let his depression affect our son's life as little as possible, I made the bed into a built-in so that he would take up less room in our home on the days he was incapable of getting out of bed or doing anything but sleeping, I encouraged him to save whatever energy he had for Hendrik whenever possible. I took care of him, but that only made him increasingly distraught. He often lashed out at me, accused me of looking down on him, of not loving him, of only putting up with him as I'd put up with a sick dog. I denied and denied it until the day I couldn't find it in me to object anymore, and told him he was right. I said I wanted a separation. He said he would kill himself. It took many more months before I found it in me to tell him that I wasn't stopping him."

Sev is silent as the main course is served. Now she has David's full attention. Then she goes on.

"One day, a year after we broke up, when he was doing a bit better and had more visitation days with our son, I came to pick Hendrik up. Peeking in through the window I saw the two of them sitting on the floor dressed as Indians, sporting these gigantic homemade feather headdresses. I knocked on the window. Ernst jumped, he'd forgotten what time it was."

"Jeez." David is looking concerned.

"Yeah. That was great."

"Great?"

"Yeah."

They eat. They drink.

"That's why, I think."

"What do you mean, that's why?" asks David.

"That's why I wanted it this way, no expectations, no obligations, no caretaking, no responsibility, no getting too comfortable, no domesticity."

"How is he doing now?"

"Oh, very much better. I think I'd completely lost what it's about, what it is, love, how it's supposed to work, whether it's important for me to finally tell you something about myself."

They eat the thinly sliced meat fanned out on their plates, the roasted beets with hazelnuts, the green salad, the fries.

"I'm sorry."

"What for?" she asks after a while.

"I'm just not ready for it."

"For what?"

"For a relationship."

"No, me neither, but that's what makes it so great. What's a relationship?"

"Hmm."

"I don't know if relationships, the way they generally turn out, turn out the way they do because it's a law of nature, or if it's just that we're all trying to follow the same model. What part is written in stone, and what part is just thoughtlessness, laziness?

How hard-and-fast is this? Can't we do it over, in a completely different way?"

He wants to get out of there, he wants to scurry back to his lair, he wants to shut the doors behind him and take care of his children as an animal tends its young. Or else back to Sev's bed, and disappear in her arms. He stares at her face, which is both strange and familiar to him.

"David?"

"Yes."

"What's up?"

"I don't know."

He finishes his meal, he doesn't like wasting food. He even stabs his fork into a piece of meat on Sev's plate; apparently she doesn't mind wasting food. When the waiter returns to clear the plates, he orders another glass of wine. He brushes the breadcrumbs on the table into a little mound. Then he looks at her.

"Hey. Are we ... are we, you know, are we still going back to your place?"

"I wanted to take a completely different tack this time, a different path from the well-trodden one, the one that means first trying like mad to shrink the distance between you, and then frantically pretending not to see the abyss."

What is she saying?

"It's been great, I've been very happy at times, the sex was good, really good, it was wonderful, uninhibited, it's incredible that you have that in you, the more troubled you are, the more fun you are, more real, more alive; but now I see you slowly slipping back into your mold, the man-mold you managed to crawl out of for a while, or got prodded out of, maybe that's a better way of putting it."

"It's been great?"

"Yes."

She's expecting him to live up to some standard, he thinks, some impossible standard, he's supposed to understand this, all these words, more words than Sev has spoken in all the past six months. Easy for her to call it a "mold"; she doesn't get it, that he can't afford to have a real affair. Now David has tears in his eyes. She does too. And as the waiter puts the plate with the candies and the check on the table between them, hers fall onto the crumpled-up napkin in front of her.

"So?"

"No," says Sev. "So, no."

"No?"

"No."

"Not back to your place, you mean?"

"Yes: no. So this really *was* the last time."

Thanks

Thanks to everyone at Uitgeverij Van Oorschot, my publisher, for making this book possible, thanks especially to Menno Hartman for your faith and your commitment. Thanks to my dear readers Laura Minderhoud, Froukje van der Ploeg, Barbara Nieuwkoop, Herman Verbeek and Marc Warning. Thanks to Matin van Veldhuizen, who sustained me from the first step to the last with questions, ideas and encouragement.

In the summer of 2017, a number of the characters in this book appeared in three linked short stories in *De Groene Amsterdammer*, *Das Magazin* and *De Gids*.

HESTER VELMANS was born in Amsterdam, but lived in five different countries while growing up, before finally settling in the US. She is the author of the popular children's books *Isabel of the Whales* and *Jessaloup's Song*. The recipient of an NEA Translation Fellowship in 2014, she was previously awarded the Vondel Prize for her translation of Renate Dorrestein's *A Heart of Stone*. Her most recent novel, *Slipper*, was published in 2018.

On the Design

As book design is an integral part of the reading experience, we would like to acknowledge the work of those who shaped the form in which the story is housed.

Tessa van der Waals (Netherlands) is responsible for the cover design, cover typography, and art direction of all World Editions books. She works in the internationally renowned tradition of Dutch Design. Her bright and powerful visual aesthetic maintains a harmony between image and typography and captures the unique atmosphere of each book. She works closely with internationally celebrated photographers, artists, and letter designers. Her work has frequently been awarded prizes for Best Dutch Book Design.

For this typographic cover, our designer Tessa van der Waals was inspired by Robert Indiana's pop art and the way he plays with letter placement. TT Trailers, a dynamic font, was a perfect fit. For the word "Love" in the title, the more malleable Variable TT Trailers font was used. TT Trailers was developed by Vika Usmanova, a graphic designer from St. Petersburg.

Suzan Beijer (Netherlands) is responsible for the typography and careful interior book design of all World Editions titles.

The text on the inside covers and the press quotes are set in Circular, designed by Laurenz Brunner (Switzerland) and published by Swiss type foundry Lineto.

All World Editions books are set in the typeface Dolly, specifically designed for book typography. Dolly creates a warm page image perfect for an enjoyable reading experience. This typeface is designed by Underware, a European collective formed by Bas Jacobs (Netherlands), Akiem Helmling (Germany), and Sami Kortemäki (Finland). Underware are also the creators of the World Editions logo, which meets the design requirement that "a strong shape can always be drawn with a toe in the sand."